What's For Dinner?

and other stories

Text illustrations by
Jacqui Thomas

Hodder & Stoughton

LONDON SYDNEY AUCKLAND

ACKNOWLEDGMENTS

The Federation of Children's Book Groups and Hodder & Stoughton Publishers are grateful to the Authors and original Publishers for permission to reproduce the stories in this collection.

British Library Cataloguing in Publication Data
A Catalogue record for this book is available from the British Library

Copyright in this collection © The Federation of Children's Book Groups 1993
Illustrations copyright © 1993 by Jacqui Thomas
Cover illustration copyright © 1991 by Mick Inkpen

The Cost of Night by Joan Aiken was first published by Lutterworth Press in *A Small Pinch of Weather*. Copyright © Joan Aiken. *Georgiana and the Dragon* by Judy Corbalis was first published by André Deutsch Ltd in *The Wrestling Princess and other stories*. Copyright © 1986 by Judy Corbalis. *Storm* by Kevin Crossley-Holland was first published by Wiliam Heinemann Limited. Copyright © 1985 by Kevin Crossley-Holland. *Harvey Angell* by Diana Hendry was firt published by Julia MacRae. Copyright © 1991 by Diana Hendry. *The Guard Dog* by Dick King-Smith was first published by Viking in *Guardian Angels*. Copyright © 1987 by Dick King-Smith. *Burper and the Magic Lamp* by Robert Leeson was first published in *An Oxford Book of Christmas Stories*, published by Oxford University Press. A shorter version was published as *Burper* by William Heinemann Limited. Copyright © 1989 by Robert Leeson. *Time Trouble* by Penelope Lively was first published by William Heinemann Limited in *Uninvited Ghosts*. Copyright © 1984 by Penelope Lively. *William's Version* by Jan Mark was first published by Penguin Books Limited in *Nothing To Be Afraid Of*. Copyright © 1980 by Jan Mark. *What's For Dinner?* by Robert Swindells was first published by Methuen Children's Books in *No More School?* Copyright © 1991 by Robert Swindells.

10 9 8 7 6 5 4 3 2

ISBN 0 340 58988 4   ISBN 0 340 58996 5 pbk

Typeset by Litho Link Ltd, Welshpool, Powys, Wales
Printed and bound in Great Britain by
Cox & Wyman Ltd, Reading, Berkshire

Hodder and Stoughton Ltd
A Division of Hodder Headline PLC
47 Bedford Square
London WC1B 3DP

Contents

The Cost of Night

by Joan Aiken
Chosen by Helen Paiba
Proprietor, The Children's Bookshop,
Muswell Hill, London

There was once a king called Merrion the Carefree who was inclined to be foolish. Perhaps this was because his wife had died when her baby daughter was born some years before, and so there was no one to keep an eye on the king. His worst failing was that he could never resist a game of chance; but of course all his subjects knew about this, and none of them would have dreamed of suggesting a game.

However it happened once that the king was returning home after a visit to a distant province of his kingdom. Towards twilight he came to a great river that was swift-flowing and wide. As he hesitated on the brink, for he was but an indifferent swimmer, he saw, moving through the reeds, an enormously large crocodile, with teeth as big as tenpins, cold expressionless yellow eyes, and a skin that looked as old and wrinkled and horny as the world itself.

'Ho, crocodile!' said King Merrion. 'I am your lord and ruler, Merrion the Carefree, so it is plainly your duty to turn crossways over the river and make a bridge, in order that I may walk dry-shod from bank to bank.'

At this the crocodile gave a great guttural choking bark, which might have been either a sardonic laugh or a respectful cough.

'Ahem, Your Majesty! I am no subject of yours, being indeed a traveller like yourself, but out of courtesy and good fellowship I don't mind making a bridge across the river for you, on one condition: that you play a game of heads or tails with me.'

Now at this point, of course, the king should have had the sense to draw back. Better if he had slept all night on the bank, or travelled upstream till he came to the next bridge, however far off it lay. But he was tired, and eager to be home; besides, at the notion of a game, all sense and caution fled out of his head.

'I'll be glad to play with you, crocodile,' he said. 'But only one quick game, mind, for I am already late and should have been home hours ago.'

So the crocodile, smiling all the way along his hundred teeth, turned sideways-on, and King Merrion walked on his horny back dry-shod from one river-bank to the other. Although the crocodile's back was covered in mud it was not slippery because of all the wrinkles.

When the king had stepped right over the hundred-tooth smile, and off the crocodile's long muddy snout, he looked about him and picked up a flat stone which was white on one side and brown on the other.

'This will do for our game, if you agree,' he said.

'Certainly I agree,' said the crocodile, smiling more than ever.

'What shall we play for?'

'The loser must grant the winner any gift he asks. You may throw first,' the crocodile said politely.

So the king threw, and the crocodile snapped, 'White!' Sure enough, the stone landed white side up.

Then the crocodile threw, and the king called, 'Brown!' But again the stone landed white side up.

Then the king threw, and again the crocodile said 'White!' and the stone landed white side up. For the fact of the matter was that the crocodile was not a genuine crocodile at all, but a powerful enchanter who chose to appear in that shape.

So the crocodile guessed right every time, and the king guessed wrong, until he was obliged to acknowledge that he had lost the game.

'What do you want for your gift?' said he.

The crocodile smiled hugely, until he looked like a tunnel through the Rocky Mountains.

'Give me,' he said, 'all the dark in your kingdom.'

At this the king was most upset. 'I am not sure that the dark is mine to give away,' he said. 'I would rather that you had asked me for all the gold in my treasury.'

'What use is gold to me?' said the crocodile. 'Remember your kingly word. The dark I want, and the dark I must have.'

'Oh, very well,' said the king, biting his lip. 'If you must, you must.'

So the crocodile opened his toothy mouth even wider, and sucked, with a suction stronger than the widest whirlpool, and all the dark in King Merrion's kingdom came rushing along and was sucked down his great cavernous throat. Indeed he sucked so hard that he swallowed up, not only the dark that covered King Merrion's country, but the dark that lay over the entire half of the world facing away from the sun, just as you might suck the pulp off a ripe plum, and he smacked his lips over it, for dark was his favourite food.

'That was delicious!' he said. 'Many thanks, Majesty! May your shadow never grow less!'

And with another loud harsh muddy laugh he disappeared.

King Merrion went home to his palace, where he

found everyone in the greatest dismay and astonishment. For instead of there being night, as would have been proper at that time, the whole country was bathed in a strange unearthly light, clear as day, but a day in which nothing cast any shadow. Flowers which had shut their petals opened them again, birds peevishly brought their heads out from under their wings, owls and bats, much puzzled, returned to their thickets, and the little princess Gudrun refused to go to bed.

Indeed, after a few days, the unhappy king realised that he had brought a dreadful trouble to his kingdom – and to the whole world – by his rash promise. Without a regular spell of dark every twelve hours, nothing went right – plants grew tall and weak and spindly, cattle and poultry became confused and stopped producing milk and eggs, winds gave up blowing, and the weather went all to pieces. As for people, they were soon in a worse muddle than the cows and hens. At first everybody tried to work all night, so as to make the most of this extra daylight, but they soon became cross and exhausted and longed for rest. However it was almost impossible to sleep, for no matter what they did, covering their windows with thick curtains, shutting their doors, hiding under the bedclothes and bandaging their eyes, not a scrap of dark could anybody find. The crocodile had swallowed it all.

As for the children, they ran wild. Bed-time had ceased to exist.

The little princess Gudrun was the first to become tired of such a state of affairs. She was very fond of listening to stories, and what she enjoyed almost more than anything else was to lie in bed with her eyes tight shut in the warm dark, and remember the fairy-tales that her nurse used to tell her. But in the hateful daylight that went on and on it was not possible to do this. So she went to confide in her greatest friend and asked his service.

Gudrun's greatest friend was a great black horse called Houniman, a battle-charger who had been sent as a gift to King Merrion several years before; battles were not very frequent at that time, so Houniman mostly roamed, grazing the palace meadows. Now Gudrun sought him out, and gave him a handful of golden corn, and tried to pretend, by burying her face in his long, thick black mane, that the dark had come again.

'What shall we do about it, Houniman?' she said.

'It is obviously no use expecting your silly father to put matters right,' Houniman replied.

'No, I am afraid you are right,' Gudrun said, sighing.

'So, as he has given away all the dark in the entire world, we shall have to find out where dark comes from and how we can get some more of it.

'But who,' she said, 'would know such a thing?'

Houniman considered, 'If we travel towards Winter,' he said at length, 'perhaps we might learn something, for in winter the dark grows until it almost swallows up the light.'

'Good,' said the princess, 'let us travel towards Winter.' So she fetched a woolly cloak, and filled her pockets with bread-and-cheese, and brought a bag of corn for Houniman, and they started out. Nobody noticed them go, since all the people in the kingdom were in such a state of muddle and upset, and King Merrion worst of all.

The princess rode on Houniman and he galloped steadily northwards for seven days and what ought to have been seven nights, over a sea of ice, until they came to the Land of Everlasting Winer, where the words freeze as you speak them, and even thoughts rattle in your head like icicles.

There they found the Lord of Winter, in the form of a great eagle, brooding on a rock.

'Sir,' called Gudrun from a good way off – for it was so cold in his neighbourhood that the very birds froze in the air and hung motionless – 'can you tell us where we can find a bit of dark?'

He lifted his head with its great hooked beak and gave them an angry look.

'Why should I help you? I have only one little piece of dark, and I am keeping it for myself, under my wing, so that it may grow.'

'Does dark grow?' said Gudrun.

'Of course it grows, stupid girl! Cark! Be off with you!' And the eagle spread one wing (keeping the other tight folded) so that a great white flurry of snow and wind drove towards Gudrun and Houniman, and they turned and galloped away.

At the edge of the Land of Winter they saw an old woman leading a reindeer loaded with wood.

'Mother,' called Gudrun, 'can you tell us where we might find a bit of dark?'

'Give me a piece of bread-and-cheese for myself and some corn for my beast and I will consider.'

So they gave her the bread and corn and she considered. Presently she said,

'There will be plenty of dark in the past. You should go to No Man's Land, the frontier where the present slips into the past, and perhaps you might be able to pick up a bit of dark there.'

'Good,' said the princess, 'that sounds hopeful. But in which direction does the past lie?'

'Towards the setting sun, of course!' snapped the old woman, and she gave her reindeer a thump to make it jog along faster.

So Gudrun and Houniman turned towards the setting sun and galloped on for seven days and what should have been seven nights, until they reached No Man's Land. This was a strange and misty region, with low hills and marshes; in the middle of it they came to a great lake, on the shore of which sat an old poet in a little garden of cranberry shrubs. Instead of water the lake was filled with blue-grey mist, and the old poet was drawing out the mist in long threads, and twisting them and turning them into poems. It was very silent all around there, with not a living creature, and the old poet was so absorbed in what he did that he never lifted his head until they stood beside him.

'Can you tell us, uncle poet,' said Gudrun, 'where we might pick up a bit of dark?'

'Dark?' he said absently. 'Eh, what's that? You want a bit of dark? There's plenty at the bottom of the lake.'

So Gudrun dismounted and walked to the edge of the lake, and looked down through the mist. Thicker and thicker it grew, darker and darker, down in the depths of the lake, and as she looked down she could see all manner of strange shapes, and some that seemed familiar too – faces that she had once known, places that she had once visited, all sunk down in the dark depths of the past. As she leaned over, the mist seemed to rise up around her, so that she began to become sleepy, to forget who she was and what she had come for . . .

'Gudrun! Come back!' cried Houniman loudly, and he stretched out his long neck and caught hold of her by the hair and pulled her back, just as she was about to topple into the lake.

'Climb on my back and let's get out of here!' he said. 'Dark or no dark, this place is too dangerous!'

But Gudrun cried to the poet, 'Uncle poet, isn't there any other place where we might pick up a bit of dark?'

'Dark?' he said. 'You want a bit of dark? Well I suppose you might try the Gates of Death; dark grows around there.'

'Where are the Gates of Death?'

'You must go to the middle of the earth, where the sky hangs so low that it is resting on the ground, and the rivers run uphill. There you will find the Gates of Death.'

And he went back to his poem-spinning.

So they galloped on for seven days and what should have been seven nights, until the mountains grew higher and higher, and the sky hung lower and lower, and at last they came to the Gates of Death.

This place was so frightening that Gudrun's heart went small inside her, because everything seemed to be turning into something else. The sky was dropping into the mountains, and the mountains piercing into the sky. A great river ran uphill, boiling, and in

front of the Gates of Death themselves a huge serpent lay coiled, with one yellow eye half open, watching as they drew near.

'Cousin serpent,' called Gudrun, trying not to let her teeth chatter, 'can you tell us where we might pick up a little piece of dark?'

'Ssss! Look about you, stupid girl!' hissed the serpent.

When Gudrun looked about her she saw that the ground was heaving and shuddering as if some great live creature were buried underneath, and there were cracks and holes in the rock, through which little tendrils of dark came leaking out.

But as fast as they appeared, the serpent snapped them off and gobbled them up.

Gudrun stretched out her hand to pick an uncurling frond of dark.

Sssstop!' hissed the serpent, darting out his head till she drew back her hand in a fright. 'All this dark is mine! And since my brother the crocodile ate all the dark in the world I will not part with one sprig of it, unless you give me something in return.'

'But what can I give you?' said Gudrun, trembling.

'You can give me your black horse. He is the colour of night, he will do very well for a tasty bite. Give him to me and you may pick one sprig of dark.'

'No, no, I cannot give you Houniman,' cried Gudrun weeping. 'He belongs to my father, not to me, and besides, he is my friend! I could not let him suffer such a dreadful fate. Take me instead, and let Houniman carry the dark back to my father's kingdom.'

'*You* wouldn't do at all,' hissed the serpent. 'You

have golden hair and blue eyes, you would give me indigestion. No, it must be the horse, or I will not part with any dark. But you must take off his golden shoes, or they will give me hiccups.'

And Houniman whispered to the princess, 'Do as the serpent says, for I have a notion that all will come right. But take care to keep my golden shoes.'

So Gudrun wiped the tears from her eyes and Houniman lifted each foot in turn while she pulled off his golden shoes. And she put them in her pockets while the serpent sucked with a great whistling noise and sucked in Houniman, mane, tail and all.

Then Gudrun picked one little sprig of dark and ran weeping away from the Gates of Death. She ran on until she was tired, and then she turned and looked back. What was her horror to see that the serpent had uncoiled himself and was coming swiftly after her. 'For,' he had thought to himself, 'I merely told her that she could *pick* one sprig in exchange for the horse, I did not say that she could carry it away. It would be a pity to waste a good sprig.' So he was coming over the rocky ground, faster than a horse could gallop.

Quick as thought, Gudrun took one of the gold horseshoes out of her pocket and flung it so that it fell over the serpent, pinning him to the rock. Twist and writhe as he might, he could not get free, and she was able to run on until he was left behind.

She passed through No Man's Land, but she was careful not to go too near the lake of mist. And she passed through the Land of Everlasting Winter, where the eagle sat guarding his little bit of dark.

Then she came to the sea of ice, but now spring was coming, and the ice was beginning to melt.

'How shall I get over to the sea?' Gudrun wondered. 'Oh, how I wish my dear Houniman were here to advise me.'

But then she remembered the gold horseshoes and thought they might help. So she pulled another from her pocket, and directly she did so it spread and stretched and turned into a boat. So Gudrun stepped into it, all the time hugging the little sprig of dark carefully against her heart, and the boat carried her safe across the sea.

Then she came to the borders of her father's kingdom, but it was still a long and weary way to his palace. For the journey that on Houniman's back had lasted only three times seven days and what should have been nights, took much longer on foot, and it was almost a year since she had left the Gates of Death. But the little sprig of dark had been growing and growing all the time.

Now Gudrun came to a wide, swift river.

In the reeds by the edge lay a crocodile, and he watched her approach with his yellow expressionless eyes.

'Ho there, little princess,' he said. 'I will play a game of heads or tails with you. If you win, I will turn my length across the river to make a bridge for you. And if I win, you shall give me the sprig of dark that you carry.'

But Gudrun did not share her father's fondness for games of chance.

'Thank you,' she said to the crocodile, 'but I have a bridge of my own.'

And she took out her third horseshoe, which immediately grew into a golden bridge, over which she crossed, leaving the crocodile to gnash his teeth with rage.

Gudrun ran on, slower and slower, for by now she was very tired, and the sprig of dark she carried had grown to the size of a young tree. But at last she reached her father's palace, and all the people ran out, with King Merrion in front, clapping their hands for joy.

'She had brought back the dark! Our darling princess has brought back the dark!'

'You must plant it in a safe, warm place and cherish it,' said Gudrun faintly. 'For I am afraid that the serpent and the crocodile may still come after it.'

So it was planted in the palace garden, and it slowly grew bigger and bigger – first as big as a nut tree, then big as a young birch, then big as a spreading oak. And King Merrion's subjects took turns to guard it, and Gudrun stayed beside it always.

But one day the envious crocodile came creeping along, in the shadow thrown by the tree of dark. The man set to guard the tree was almost asleep, for the shadow made him drowsy after so many months of daylight, but Gudrun saw the crocodile.

Quick as a flash she pulled out her fourth horseshoe and threw it, pinning the crocodile to the ground.

But then she grew very anxious, 'For,' she said, 'what shall we do if the serpent comes? Now I have no more horseshoes! Oh, my dear, good, faithful friend Houniman, how I do miss you!'

And she laid her head against the trunk of the tree and wept bitter tears.

Now this watering was just what the tree needed, and that very minute it grew and flourished until its branches spread right across the sky and true night had come at last. Directly this happened, all the creatures of night who had stayed sulking in their hiding-places for so long, the owls and moths and night-herons, the bats, bitterns, nightjars and nightingales, and all the beasts of darkness, came out rejoicing and calling down blessings on the little princess Gudrun. But she still knelt weeping beside the tree.

Then the king of the night creatures, who was an enormous owl, looked down with his great eyes and saw the serpent creeping through the dark. (In the end, after many days, he had managed to wriggle out from under the horseshoe.)

'Thief, thief!' cried the owl. 'Kill him! Kill him!' And all the creatures of dark flew down, pecking and tearing, until they had pecked the serpent in a thousand pieces. And out of the pieces sprang Houniman, alive and well!

Then Gudrun flung her arms round Houniman's neck and wept for joy, and King Merrion offered him any reward he cared to name for helping to bring back dark to the world.

'All I ask,' said Houniman, 'is that you set me free, for in my own land, far to the east, where night begins, I was king and lord over all the wild horses.'

'Willingly will I grant what you ask,' said King Merrion. So Houniman was given his freedom and he bade a loving farewell to the princess Gudrun and galloped away and away, home to his own country. But he sent back his son, the black colt, Gandufer, to be the princess's lifelong companion and friend.

The creatures of night offered to peck the crocodile to pieces too, but King Merrion said no to that.

'I shall keep him a prisoner always, and the sight of him will be a reminder to me never again to get mixed up in a game of chance!' he said.

And so this was done.

Georgiana and the Dragon

by Judy Corbalis

Chosen by Fiona Waters

Editorial Director, School Book Fairs Ltd

Once upon a time in a far country, there lived a king in a golden palace. The palace had television in every room, a soda fountain in the billiard room, and in the throne room an icecream-making machine which could produce one hundred and forty-seven different flavoured icecreams. All the waterfalls in the palace gardens were made of lemonade, and the mud at the edges was chocolate.

The king had one child, his daughter, the Princess Georgiana. She had red hair and green eyes, and a very hot temper, and she loved playing football and doing daring unusual things, whenever she could find any to do.

The king should have been very happy, but he had one serious problem. His kingdom was being terrorised by a huge dragon which had suddenly flown in a year before and had settled in a cave on the top of a hill thirteen miles from the palace. The king knew the cave very well indeed because he had had a treasure hoard hidden there just in case he should ever need it, and now the dragon was in the cave guarding the treasure and making it impossible for the king to get it back.

'The whole situation's hopeless,' sighed the king to his Lord Chamberlain.

'It does seem so, Your Majesty,' agreed the Lord Chamberlain.

'And,' went on the king tragically, 'as if that's not bad enough, the wretched beast has taken to going out from time to time and breathing on the crops and forests and burning them up. Three of the peasants have lost their houses as well. Everybody's getting very fed up and they're all expecting *me* to do something about it.'

'Well, you *are* the king, after all. It's only natural they should look to you for help,' murmured the respectful Lord Chamberlain.

'I don't see that at all.' The king was belligerent. 'It's certainly my bad luck but that doesn't make it my responsibility.'

The Lord Chamberlain was firm.

'Well, the people see it that way, Your Majesty. And if Your Majesty wants to keep their loyalty and support, and remain a much-loved monarch . . .'

'All right, all right,' muttered the king. 'So what should I do about it?'

'With respect . . .' began the Lord Chamberlain.

'Forget the respect,' said the king testily. 'And get on with the ideas. And quickly.'

The Lord Chamberlain quietly ground his teeth together and went on.

'As I was saying, what Your Majesty needs is a contest.'

'A contest?'

'To find a young prince to kill the dragon and free the people from their worries about it and the bonfires it creates, and also to release Your Majesty's treasure.'

'It's a good idea in theory,' said the king, 'but in practice, I can't think of any princes, or even knights, come to that, who'd be crazy enough to do it. That dragon breathes fire.'

'Exactly,' said the Lord Chamberlain, 'which is why Your Majesty is offering a large reward. It's called an incentive,' he explained.

'But I'm not offering one,' said the king, puzzled.

'You must, Your Majesty,' replied the Lord Chamberlain. 'Or none of them will agree to try.'

'What shall I offer?' said the king.

'In these cases,' said the Lord Chamberlain, 'it's usual to offer the hand of the Princess in marriage and half your kingdom.'

'HALF MY KINGDOM!' The king was outraged. 'That's insane.'

'But necessary,' assured the Lord Chamberlain.

'A quarter then,' said the king sulkily.

'No, a quarter's too little,' said the Lord Chamberlain. 'Perhaps a third now and the rest when Your Majesty is no longer with us. Which, of course, we hope will not be for many, many years yet,' he added hastily, noticing the king's expression.

'Well, as you say I've got no choice,' said the king, 'I'll obviously have to do it. But I don't like it, I can tell you.'

'Since Your Majesty's mind is now made up, I'll go off and draw up a set of rules for the contest and broadcast the news of the competition,' said the Lord Chamberlain.

And he rushed off before the king could change his mind.

The king went moodily over to the icecream machine and ordered himself a treble bubblegum, wild strawberry and Chinese king prawn icecream with a giant flake. Some time later, as he was finishing it, the Lord Chamberlain came back.

'I've drawn up the rules,' he announced, 'and I've posted notices of the contest all over the place, and sent messengers off to all four corners of the kingdom to put up notices and spread the word.'

20

'How long will that take?' asked the king.

'About an hour or two,' said the Lord Chamberlain. 'Three, at most. They all went on trail bikes.'

By nightfall, fourteen knights and three princes had registered as contestants.

'I wish there were more princes,' sighed the king.

'There might be. More may apply tomorrow,' pointed out the Lord Chamberlain. 'But I must remind Your Majesty that princes are in short supply. Really, I'm surprised that as many as three have entered.'

'Prince Blanziflor's on the register, I see,' said the king. 'I'm pleased about that. His mother's an old friend of mine. I think he should try first. If I have to give up some of my kingdom, I don't mind so much if it's Blanziflor who wins it.'

'He has to slay the dragon first,' murmured the Lord Chamberlain.

In the next morning's mail bag there were another five applications.

'Superb,' said the king. 'We shall start tomorrow.'

And he ordered a large canopy to be put up and invited all the people to watch a display by the princes and knights before they set off.

'They can stay in the palace until it's their own turn,' he explained to the Lord Chamberlain and the Court Jester, 'and we will have entertainments every night for them.'

The jester hurried away looking pleased. He liked showing off at entertainments.

The following afternoon the dragon slayers assembled on their horses in the palace yard. From under the canopy a large crowd watched them, impressed. In the special royal box in the centre sat the Princess Georgiana and behind her sat the rest of the palace staff. The princess looked interestedly at the competitors.

'I hope the dragon gets them all,' she remarked to the Lord Chamberlain.

'Your Highness!' The Lord Chamberlain was shocked.

'Well, I don't want to marry any of *them*,' said the princess. 'I don't even think much of their horses.'

There was a scuffle at the portcullis. It was raised. The king peered out.

'Who is it?'

'It's me,' gasped a voice, and in on a large white horse rode a rather scruffy looking prince in a football shirt.

'Prince Blanziflor, Your Majesty,' he announced to the king, jumping off his horse and bowing low. A large guitar case was strapped on the back of his saddle.

'I got lost,' he explained, 'I'm sorry I'm late.'

'You're just in time,' said the king. 'I know your mother. How is she?'

'Rather upset, I'm afraid,' said Blanziflor. 'She's very worried that I'll be eaten by the dragon. I *am* her only son, you see. But, on the other hand, times are hard and there aren't many kingdoms going begging at present, and it did seem a good opportunity . . .'

'Quite,' said the king. 'Naturally. Of course. Well,' he went on, ushering Prince Blanziflor into the courtyard, 'you're here now, and that's what counts.'

'I say,' said Prince Blanziflor, looking up. 'Is that

the princess? She looks rather nice.' And he waved.

The Princess Georgiana waved back.

'Who's that?' she asked the Lord Chamberlain.

'Prince Blanziflor, I think,' said the Lord Chamberlain.

'I hope the dragon doesn't eat *him*,' said the princess thoughtfully.

The dragon-slayers' pageant began. The crowds cheered and applauded as the young princes and knights rode up and down the courtyard in their armour. When it was finally over, the king lit the bonfire for the royal fireworks display. The Princess Georgiana was watching the Catherine wheels and rockets when she felt a tap on her shoulder. She turned around.

'I say,' said an eager voice, 'I've been trying to meet you for ages. Hello.'

'Hello!' said the princess. 'Who are you?'

'I'm Prince Blanziflor.'

'I'm the Princess Georgiana.'

'I know,' said the prince. 'You look as if you're good fun. Can you play football?'

'I love it!' cried the princess. 'If you sneak round the back with me we could kick a few balls secretly now whilst no one's looking.'

'Oh yes!' said the prince.

He took her hand and together they crept away from the crowd and out onto the palace football pitch. They had been practising goals for quite some time when the princess said suddenly,

'What time is it?'

'I don't know,' answered the prince. 'I haven't got a watch. But it's quite late.'

'Oh dear,' said the Princess Georgiana, 'I'm supposed to be at the banquet.'

'So am I!' said the prince.

'But I'm the guest of honour.'

'Well,' said Blanziflor, 'we'll just have to go in together and hope no one notices.'

They went back to the palace entrance and slipped into the banqueting hall. The king looked up from the end of the golden table.

'Where have *you* been?' he said severely to his daughter.

'Oh, Papa . . .' began the princess, but Prince Blanziflor said loudly, 'I'm terribly sorry, Your Majesty, I asked your daughter to show me the palace maze and I'm afraid we got lost.'

'You seem to make a habit of getting lost,' remarked the king. 'Well, now that you both *are* here, you'd better sit down and start eating.'

The Princess Georgiana sat on her father's right hand. Prince Blanziflor sat near the bottom of the table.

At the end of the meal the king rose and gave a speech of welcome and thanks to all the competitors. Then he announced, 'The Lord Chamberlain has drawn lots to see who will have the first chance of meeting the dragon, and here is the list of princes and knights in the order they will go off to fight.

'First, Prince Belvedere.

Second, the Star Green Knight.

Third . . .'

He droned on until the princess heard,

'Seventeenth, Prince Blanziflor.'

'Maybe, by then,' she thought, 'the dragon will be

badly wounded and Prince Blanziflor will succeed.'

The banquet finished, and after drinking one another's health, everyone retired to bed.

The next day, to the accompaniment of great cheers, Prince Belvedere set off to fight the dragon.

The king's messenger returned the day after with unhappy news.

'I'm afraid, Sire, Prince Belvedere has perished.'

In quick succession followed four knights and two more princes.

'Your Majesty,' said the Lord Chamberlain, several days later, after the palace messenger had reported the sixteenth competitor frizzled up by dragon's breath or fatally wounded by dragon's claws, 'is it sensible to continue?'

'As I recall,' said the king, 'this was *your* idea, not mine, so it's on your head, I'm afraid.'

'The next contestant,' announced the court usher, 'has come to say farewell, Your Majesty. Prince Blanziflor.'

The prince came jauntily into the throne room and sank on one knee.

'Your blessing, Sire,' he murmured humbly.

'Good luck, my boy,' said the king kindly. 'And I hope you get my treasure back.'

'And may I have *your* blessing, Your Highness,' said Prince Blanziflor, bending low in front of the Princess Georgiana.

'Granted,' replied the princess graciously. 'And I have a piece of advice for you.'

And she whispered in his ear, 'If in doubt, give in and run.'

Prince Blanziflor bowed and left.

Twelve hours later the king's messenger re-appeared.

'Terrible news, Your Majesty. Prince Blanziflor has been taken prisoner by the dragon. He is being held hostage in the dragon's cave.'

'How shocking!' cried the king. 'We must send another contestant to rescue him.'

'Impossible!' said the Lord Chamberlain. 'There were only five more competitors, and they've all resigned. There's no one left to rescue him. You will have to go yourself, Sire.'

'I'd love to go, of course,' said the king, 'but, unfortunately, I'm too old.'

'Well, I don't know what we can do, Sire,' said the Lord Chamberlain.

'His mother will be awfully cross,' said the king thoughtfully.

'Undoubtedly, Sire.'

'Are you sure there are no more contestants?'

'None at all, Sire,' the Lord Chamberlain assured him.

They sat together for some time, thinking deeply.

The door opened and the Princess Georgiana came in.

'Yes, my dear?' asked the king.

'I've come to register,' said the princess.

'Register?' The king was puzzled.

'For the contest.'

The king looked even more puzzled. 'What contest?'

'Really, Papa!' sighed the princess. You *are* impossible. The dragon slaying contest, of course. I want to kill the dragon.'

'Georgiana!' cried the king. 'Don't be ridiculous. You can't possibly kill the dragon. I've never heard such nonsense.'

'I *can* kill the dragon,' said the princess calmly. '*And* rescue Prince Blanziflor. And I've come to register. Can you put my name down, please?' she asked, turning to the Lord Chamberlain. 'I want to be a contestant.'

'Well, you can't,' said the king firmly. 'It has to be a prince who slays the dragon.'

'It doesn't say so in the rules,' objected the princess.

'It does,' said the Lord Chamberlain.

'Where, then?' demanded the princess.

The Lord Chamberlain took up the parchment scroll. He read it through very thoroughly, then re-read it. He was on the third re-read when the king said, nastily, 'Well, come on, read it aloud.'

The Lord Chamberlain cleared his throat.

'I can't actually find it, Your Majesty.'

'See!' said the princess triumphantly.

The king looked hard at the Lord Chamberlain.

'What do you mean, you can't find it? I thought it was rule fifty-three.'

'With respect, Your Majesty,' mumbled the Lord Chamberlain, 'rule fifty-three is to do with claims of compensation in the event of death by dragon's breath.'

'I told you it wasn't in the rules,' said the princess, 'so I'm going.'

'It's unfeminine,' said the king. 'No one's ever heard of a princess fighting a dragon.'

'They will have after I've done it,' said the princess.

The king sighed heavily.

'I wonder if commoners have these troubles,' he remarked to the ceiling.

'Undoubtedly, Sire,' cried the Lord Chamberlain and the Court Jester simultaneously.

'Not much consolation,' said the king.

And to the princess he said, 'Well, under the circumstances I don't suppose I can stop you.'

'I'll need a longbow, this list of equipment and a red suit of armour,' said the princess. 'Do you think someone could get them for me by morning, please? Oh, and a banner, of course.'

'I'll see to it myself,' said the Lord Chamberlain, and he hurried away.

'Georgiana,' said the king, 'let me explain it to you once more. That dragon is ferocious and desperate. It's guarding a priceless treasure and it will stop at nothing to keep it. It has Prince Blanziflor imprisoned at the back of its cave; it's already sizzled up some of the knights and princes and frightened off the rest of them. This is a doomed enterprise.'

'I'm going and that's that,' said the princess in an even more determined tone.

The king looked resigned.

'I've tried to stop you,' he said. 'I've explained the dangers and, of course, you *are* my only daughter and I love you dearly, but if you won't listen to reason and you want to upset me and cause me grief and woe, go right ahead.'

'That's emotional blackmail, Papa,' said the Princess Georgiana. 'You should be ashamed of yourself. And there won't be any grief or woe: you'll be rejoicing because the dragon's slain.'

'Nobody's going to slay that dragon,' answered the king. 'How can they? It's impossible.'

'I don't think so,' said Georgiana, and then, with a sudden surge of enthusiasm, she asked, 'Do you think, as it might be my last meal for ages, we could have passion-fruit layer cake for supper?'

'It might be your last meal ever, so I suppose we'd better,' said the king moodily. 'Order it from Cook. But I won't enjoy it much, I can tell you.'

Princess Georgiana set off for the kitchen. On the way she met the Lord Chamberlain.

'Your Highness,' began the Lord Chamberlain.

'Yes?'

'It's about your heraldic emblem. What creature would you like emblazoned on your shield? All the knights have an animal or bird or heraldic beast of some kind.'

The princess thought for a bit. Then she said, 'A gerbil, I think. I like gerbils.'

'I'm not really sure that a gerbil is quite suitable,' said the Lord Chamberlain.

'Well, it's what I want,' answered the princess cheerily and she sped away to the kitchen.

The princess got up next morning, dressed in her new red armour which the maid had laid out ready for her, and went down to breakfast. Crowds of people were assembling outside the palace to watch her set off. She collected her equipment and her sandwiches, brushed her teeth thoroughly with her golden toothbrush, kissed the king and went outside.

The people cheered loudly and she gave a gracious wave as she jumped into her red sports car with the golden gerbil emblem on each door and the small gold crown on top, and set off. Behind her came a groom driving the royal horsebox with her horse, Bucephalus, inside.

About two miles from the dragon's cave the princess pulled up. The horse-box stopped behind her and the groom got out.

'You can get the horse ready now,' said the princess carelessly. 'I can see smoke on the horizon. It must be the dragon.'

'I expect so, Your Highness,' said the groom nervously, and he began to open the horse-box. He paused, 'Your horse may not like the smoke,' he pointed out.

'Bucephalus isn't frightened of *anything*. I trained him myself.'

'Will Your Highness actually be needing me,' asked the groom, 'or will it be all right for me to go back to the palace?'

'Oh, you can go back,' the princess assured him. 'I can manage quite well by myself.'

The groom saluted nervously. He set up the mounting steps. 'Thank you, ma'am,' he said with relief.

And he tied Bucephalus to a nearby tree, shut up the royal horse-box and jumped in behind the steering wheel.

Two seconds later he was out again. 'Good luck, Your Highness.'

'Oh thanks,' said the princess and she waved to him as he drove away.

Bucephalus whinnied and lifted his head. The Princess Georgiana stroked his neck.

'Good boy,' she said soothingly, and she untied the reins, climbed onto the mobile steps (because she was quite heavy in her armour) and got onto his back.

'Here we go,' said the Princess Georgiana, and they set off to meet the dragon.

They had not gone far when the smoke began to get thicker and the air felt warmer.

'Thank goodness I had special heatproof armour made,' thought the princess.

They rode on. As they approached the hill where the dragon was guarding the cave, they could hear the sounds of a guitar.

'It must be Prince Blanziflor at the back of the cave. I expect that's how he passes the time,' said the princess.

Bucephalus snorted.

Flames were shooting out of the cave entrance. The Princess Georgiana smiled to herself and thought contentedly of the fire extinguisher strapped to her sword case.

At the bottom of the hill she stopped, jumped down from Bucephalus's back and tied him to a large rock.

'Wait there like a good horse,' she told him kindly, and patted his nose.

Bucephalus nuzzled her.

Princess Georgiana set off on foot up the hill to meet the dragon.

There was a rumble and a roar! The ground shook. Out of the cave poked a huge dragon's head.

'What do you want,' it growled nastily.

The Princess smiled. 'I've come sightseeing,' she answered.

'Sightseeing!' snarled the dragon. 'What do you mean? Sightseeing.'

'I've come to see the dragon.'

'I *am* the dragon,' said the dragon proudly. 'I terrorise the neighbourhood round here. I've frizzled up princes and knights with my hot breath already, and I've got a prince trapped in my cave. As a matter of fact,' it went on confidentially, 'I'm guarding a priceless treasure in there.'

'You're not!' The Princess Georgiana was disbelieving.

'Oh yes, I am,' said the dragon, and it spat nastily at her. A long flame shot out of its mouth.

'Could you do that again, please?' asked the princess.

'Why?'

'I just wondered if you could.'

'Of course I can,' said the dragon boastfully, and it shot out another sheet of flame.

'How nice,' said the princess. She undid her quiver and took out a long toasting fork and a bag of marshmallows.

'Now, I'll just sit here with my fork and toast marshmallows on your breath, if you don't mind.'

'Well, I'm not actually doing anything special right now, so I suppose I could,' agreed the dragon.

They sat for some time while the princess toasted and ate marshmallows.

'I don't believe you've really got a prince in there,' said Princess Georgiana.

'I have.' The dragon was confident.

'Well, where is he then?'

'I don't let him *out*,' said the dragon scornfully. 'He

might run away. He's my hostage. He's playing the guitar in there now.'

'I see,' said the princess. 'Where exactly have you put him?'

'He's right at the back of the cave.'

'Oh.'

She took another marshmallow from her bag, pushed it onto her fork and held it in front of the dragon.

'Blow again, please.'

The dragon was irritated. 'Look here,' it rumbled. 'I've got better things to do all day than sit about toasting things for silly girls.'

'I'm not a silly girl,' said the Princess Georgiana. 'I'm actually very clever and strong *and* can tap-dance.'

'In full armour? I don't believe it,' said the dragon.

'Of course, I can't tap-dance in my *armour*.'

'And come to that,' went on the dragon, 'what are you doing in full armour anyway? Whoever heard of anyone sightseeing in armour.'

The Princess Georgiana thought quickly. 'Well, I am,' she said, 'so now you have heard of somebody doing it. My mother makes me wear it. I've got a very weak chest and she thinks it will stop me from catching cold.'

'She sounds a bit over-protective,' commented the dragon.

'She is,' said the princess hastily. 'But, of course, I have to do as she says.'

'Quite right too,' answered the dragon. 'People should do as their mothers tell them.'

'Do *you*?' The princess was curious.

'Of course not,' said the dragon. 'I'm a *dragon*. Dragons don't do as they're told.'

The princess was thoughtful. 'I see.' Then she went on suddenly, 'So it wouldn't be any use telling you to stay in that cave and not follow me to see what I'm doing when I go off in a few minutes.'

'No, it would not,' said the dragon. 'Because I'll just follow you if I want to.'

'What if I *ordered* you not to follow me?'

'I don't get ordered round by anyone, especially not girls. I'd just follow you anyway. You couldn't stop me.'

'I see.'

Princess Georgiana was thoughtful. She put another marshmallow on the fork, then quickly pulled it off and ate it untoasted.

'It's a pretty day,' she remarked.

'Very,' agreed the dragon.

They sat in companionable silence for some time.

'I expect your cave's rather dismal and ugly inside,' said the princess.

The dragon was hurt. 'It's actually very well decorated,' it snapped. 'And there's a beautiful gem collection in one corner.

The princess knew all about the gem collection: she had heard her father lamenting its loss frequently.

'Oh, really,' she answered politely.

'You don't sound very impressed,' complained the dragon.

'I'm sure your gems are very beautiful,' replied the princess, 'but I don't believe you've got as many as you say. I think you're boasting.'

The dragon was furious. It roared out a cloud of

black smoke and stamped till the ground rumbled.

The guitar music inside the cave stopped.

'How dare you?' shouted the dragon. 'You ignorant girl. I'll show you if I'm boasting or not. Come inside and have a look and see if I'm telling the truth. You owe me a big apology.'

'If it's true, I'll apologise,' said the princess. 'And if it's not true, you have to.'

'IT IS TRUE!' screamed the dragon. 'Go in there and look!'

It moved to one side of the cave entrance.

The princess went cautiously forward. It was very gloomy inside. She took a deep breath and stepped past the dragon, into the dark.

At first she could see nothing at all, then, as her eyes adjusted to the gloom, she noticed a faint glow at the very back of the cave. She moved towards it. As she drew nearer, she realised the glow came from an enormous heap of coloured stones.

'My goodness,' breathed the princess to herself, 'it must be the gem collection! But it can't be. It's enormous.'

She looked hard. Diamonds, rubies, emeralds, sapphires, turquoises, opals and bars of gold and silver sparkled and gave off a soft warm light.

'Amazing!' sighed the princess aloud.

'I know,' whispered a voice beside her.

'Prince Blanziflor!' said the princess.

She had forgotten all about him in the excitement of going into the dark cave.

'Ssh, quietly,' he hissed. 'The dragon has super-acute hearing. Don't let it hear you talking to me. I *am* Prince Blanziflor and I've been trapped here for ages.

Can you get someone to free me?'

'I've come to free you,' whispered the Princess Georgiana.

'Good Heavens, it's Princess Georgiana! You free me?' The prince stifled a giggle. 'Why, you're a girl!'

'I'm a princess actually,' said Georgiana huffily, 'and if you don't want to be rescued that's fine with me. Just let me know and I'll leave straightaway.'

'Oh no, please.' The prince was humble. 'I'm sorry. I don't care who rescues me, as long as I get out of here. I can only play three tunes on the guitar and I'm sick to death of them, and all that dragon gives me to eat is porridge. Can you imagine it?' he went on gloomily. 'Porridge, porridge, porridge, three times a day. It's awful.'

'You're luckly the dragon hasn't killed you,' said the princess. 'Why doesn't it?'

'It thinks I'm too useful as a hostage,' explained the prince. 'But I don't see how you're going to rescue me. There's no chance. It's killed the others already.'

'I know,' said the princess. 'I say, I think I might just slip a diamond in my quiver and take it with me.'

'Don't, don't!' Prince Blanziflor was very agitated. 'You mustn't. The last time that happened it burnt up the knight who did it in one breath. Just like a flame-thrower. It was terrible.'

'How awful!' whispered the princess. 'But it won't know I've taken it.'

'It will. It'll smell it,' explained the prince.

'Smell it?'

'Yes. Dragons can smell precious stones: their noses are very sensitive to gems and they can smell diamonds and rubies over fifty metres away.'

'Gosh!' The princess was impressed.

'That's how it found this treasure,' went on Prince Blanziflor. 'It was flying by and it smelt it and burned down the huge wooden doors at the cave entrance with its fiery breath and it's been here ever since, guarding it.'

'I see,' said the princess. 'Well, I won't take one now I know that.' She thought for a minute. 'I'd better go out soon or it'll get suspicious. And I've got a plan. If you want to be rescued you'll have to do as I say.' And she whispered urgently in his ear.

'Yes, I will,' muttered Prince Blanziflor. 'But do be careful, won't you?'

'No,' said the princess. 'I won't be careful: I'll be clever. See you later. And don't forget to do exactly what I told you.'

'Goodbye,' said Prince Blanziflor.

The princess went out of the cave and stood blinking in the sunlight by the entrance.

The dragon looked at her and took a deep breath.

'You didn't take anything,' it said in astonishment.

'Of course not,' answered Princess Georgiana. '*I'm* not a thief. And I owe you an apology. That's a WONDERFUL collection of jewels – the best I've ever seen.'

The dragon looked proud.

'Where did you get them?'

'I found them,' it said arrogantly. 'All by myself. I smelt them as I was flying by.'

'But didn't they belong to someone else?'

'They're mine now,' remarked the dragon.

'But that's stealing.'

The dragon was enraged.

'Shut up, shut up!' it shouted. 'I won't listen. Stop accusing me.' And it stamped and screamed. The ground rumbled.

'Honestly, you are a baby,' said the princess, unimpressed. 'Do stop it. You're making earthquakes. And I want to tell you something. You've got someone in that cave, did you know?'

'Of course I know, I told you already. It's a prince. He's my hostage.'

'Oh yes, so you did,' replied the princess. 'What do you feed him?'

'Porridge,' explained the dragon. 'It's very good for him.'

'Porridge!' The princess was incredulous. 'Seriously?'

'Yes. Why not?' the dragon was puzzled.

'Well, no reason why not,' said the Princess Georgiana, 'except I personally wouldn't waste good porridge on a hostage.'

'What do you mean?'

'It seems to me,' said the princess slowly, 'that it's a terrible waste of precious food to give porridge to a *hostage*. I wouldn't. But I suppose you can afford it with a gem collection like yours.'

'I can't, I can't. I'm terribly poor, actually,' moaned the dragon. 'It's dreadful. I haven't *any* money at all. And I can't sell my treasure. I thought he didn't like porridge and it served him right to be made to eat it.'

'Well, have it your own way, then. I don't care,' answered the princess.

'How do you mean? You must tell me. What should I feed him?'

'You can do as you want,' said the princess, 'but if

I, personally, had a hostage like that, I certainly wouldn't waste valuable porridge on him. I'd make him eat bacon and eggs every morning, and baked beans and ham and sausages and tomatoes and roast potatoes and horrible things like that.'

'But I thought he would *like* those sorts of things. I want to make life hard for him.'

The princess threw back her head and laughed and laughed.

'You are silly,' she cried. 'Fancy punishing someone by feeding him porridge. Have it your own way. Carry on, but I'll bet he loves porridge just like I do.'

'Right!' said the dragon grimly. 'No more porridge for him! From now on he gets bacon and eggs and baked beans.'

'Whatever you do, don't give him water either,' said the princess. 'Make him drink lemonade or something sickly and gassy like that.'

'All right,' said the dragon. 'And thank you. You are a help.'

'I try to be,' said the Princess Georgiana. 'And if I were you, I'd start with the baked beans now. Just watch his face when you give them to him. He'll be really upset.'

'Yes, I will,' said the dragon.

'Well, I'll be off to do some more sightseeing,' said the princess cheerily, and she got up. 'Thank you for toasting the marshmallows. Maybe I'll come back and see you tomorrow.'

'Yes, do that,' answered the dragon, 'if your mother will let you.'

'Bye,' called the Princess Georgiana.

'Bye!' shouted the dragon.

The princess set off down the hill.

She was back next morning.

'Hello!' she called loudly.

The dragon poked its head out of the cave.

'Oh, it's you.'

'I came to ask you something.'

'Well, ask me then,' grumbled the dragon, 'and hurry up about it.'

'I told my mother about you and she asked if it's true that dragons have ugly great warts on their noses.'

'Of course I don't!' snapped the dragon. 'What a rude and stupid girl you are. You can see for yourself I haven't got warts. In fact, I'm considered very handsome as dragons go.'

'People think *I'm* pretty, too,' said the Princess Georgiana.

'*I* don't,' remarked the dragon.

The Princess Georgiana ignored him and went on, 'I told my mother about your gem collection. She said it couldn't be a very big one, the way I described it. It didn't sound to her as big as the treasure the other dragon's got over at Widdock Hill in the next kingdom.'

'It's bigger and better,' screeched the dragon. 'How dare you say it's smaller? You are the most ignorant girl I ever met.'

'Well, I'd sort of forgotten it by the time I got home,' explained the princess, 'so perhaps I didn't describe it to my mother properly.'

'Go inside that cave and look again!' ordered the dragon.

The princess looked worried.

'I don't think I should.'

'You must. I'm telling you to,' snapped the dragon. 'And when you've seen it again you can tell your mother the truth. Why, it's seven times as big as that gem collection of old One-Eye at Widdock's Hill. No comparison at all.'

The princess went reluctantly into the cave.

Once she was inside she slipped to the back and whispered in Prince Blanziflor's ear.

'Did it work?'

The prince nodded.

Then he whispered back, 'The baked beans were WONDERFUL.'

'Just do as I say and trust me,' murmured the princess.

Blanziflor nodded.

The princess went back outside.

'You're right,' she said, impressed. 'It *is* enormous. I'd forgotten. I'll get on back home and tell my mother right away. 'Bye then.'

'Oh, by the way,' rumbled the dragon, 'thank you for that advice about feeding the hostage. You should have seen his face when I gave him baked beans. He hated them.'

'I'll bet he did,' said the princess, and waving goodbye she set off down the hillside.

She spent the night camped about two miles away with Bucephalus. They built a fire together.

'My armour's getting heavy,' complained the princess.

Bucephalus nodded sympathetically, as they stretched out beside each other and fell asleep.

*   *   *

Next day, the princess got up very early. She rode Bucephalus back to the bottom of the hill and tied him to the tree, out of sight. Then she checked her amour and equipment, slung her longbow on her back and went up the hill.

A short distance from the cave she stopped.

'Come out, you stupid old dragon,' she shouted. 'I'm the Princess Georgiana and I've come to fight you and claim back my father's treasure. It's not yours. You stole it. You're nothing but a thief.'

There was a low rumble and a roar from inside the cave. The ground shook.

The princess went several steps closer.

'You're afraid,' she called. 'You're too scared to fight me!'

A blast of flame came pouring out of the cave. Even from a distance the princess could feel the heat on her cheeks. She pulled down her heat proof vizor and, taking out her sword, she clashed it against a large rock.

'You're not a dragon. You're nothing but a baby.'

There was a terrible howl from the cave. The dragon came roaring out.

'It's you!' it shrieked. 'You wicked girl. I'll roast you alive.'

And it breathed out a huge double jet of flame.

The Princess Georgiana hid behind a rock. She was terrified, but she was also very brave. Fumbling at her side, she unstrapped her fire extinguisher, then, poking her head out from behind the rock, she called, 'Yah, yah, can't catch me!'

The dragon was enraged. It exhaled a mighty breath and shot out an even longer tongue of fire. Just as she felt the searing heat over her head, the princess raised the fire extinguisher and pressed the lever.

The dragon's fiery breath vanished. It coughed and choked and spat. By now it was thoroughly angry and furious.

'You won't escape me,' it bellowed and, rising on its hind legs with its wings outstretched, it showed its enormous talons. 'I'll tear you to pieces!'

It was a terrifying sight. Georgiana felt as though she was having a nightmare.

'I must be calm and sensible,' she whispered to herself, but her hands shook with fright. Trembling, she took out her catapult, spat on her hands for luck, and, with one deft move, popped a sharp stone in the sling and pulled it back.

The dragon came closer. Georgiana saw its terrible pointed teeth. She pulled the catapult sling tighter, took a deep breath and let fly. Twang!

The stone shot through the air and lodged straight in the dragon's forehead between the eyes. The dragon gave an earsplitting scream. Fiery vapour came pouring out of the wound and black blood spurted out of its mouth. It writhed and tossed and shook, then fell in a heap onto the ground.

The Princess Georgiana remembered what her old nanny had told her about dragons.

'They're very tricky things, dragons. Never let one fool you. Just when you think they're dead and done for, they jump up and catch you again.'

So she went, very cautiously, just a little nearer.

The dragon's eyes were closed and its body trembled.

'I'd better be on the safe side,' thought the princess.

She fumbled under her armour and pulling out a box of matches, took one out and struck it against her knee pads. It lit. Georgiana took a dead branch from the ground nearby and set fire to the end. Then she picked up her longbow, set the branch in like an arrow, took aim and fired the burning branch straight into the dragon's chest.

There was a tremendous explosion! A jet of flame shot into the air and enveloped the dragon. Boom! It frizzled up within a minute.

'Nanny was right then!' murmured the princess. 'Dragons *do* have liquid gas instead of blood. How lucky I wasn't standing too close.'

She went cautiously up to the crater in the ground where the dragon had been. There was nothing left but a heap of soot and ashes.

'Serves you right!' said the princess sternly. 'You wicked dragon. Well, ex-dragon, I mean.'

And she hurried up to the cave to tell Prince Blanziflor he was now free.

'You can come out,' she called. 'You're free. I've slain the dragon.'

There was a little scuffling noise from the back of the cave.

'Are you sure?' whispered a frightened voice.

'Positive!'

'But I just heard a most terrible explosion.'

'I know. It was me blowing up the dragon.'

'Was it? I thought it was the dragon blowing up *you*.'

The prince peeped cautiously out of the doorway, saw the dragon was gone, and stood blinking in the unaccustomed sunlight.

He looked at the princess. His lip trembled, he threw his arms round her neck and burst into tears.

'My heroine! How can I ever thank you enough?' he sobbed.

The Princess Georgiana patted him soothingly.

'Never mind,' she said. 'It's all over now. All we have to do is get you back to your mother's kingdom.'

Prince Blanziflor wept harder.

'I haven't even got a horse. Mine bolted when it saw the dragon.'

'We can both ride on mine,' said the princess generously. And she led him over to the tree where Bucephalus was waiting.

Blanziflor climbed up on his back, and Princess Georgiana was just about to get up too when suddenly she stopped.

'Wait,' she cried, and rushed off into the cave. She reappeared with a large piece of wood on which she wrote,

'PROPERTY OF THE PRINCESS GEORGIANA KEEP YOUR HANDS OFF!!!'

She propped it up at the cave entrance.

'We can come back later for the treasure,' she explained.

'We?' asked Prince Blanziflor.

'Me and the palace guards,' said the princess.

The prince was disappointed. 'I thought you meant me.'

'Do you want to come? I thought you hated it here.'

'It'd be different coming here with you, with no

dragon,' explained Blanziflor.

The princess smiled at him.

Prince Blanziflor took her hand.

'Will you marry me?' asked the princess.

Prince Blanziflor looked disappointed again.

'You're supposed to get down on one knee and ask me,' he pointed out.

'As a matter of fact,' snapped the princess, *you're* supposed to do the asking.' And she stamped off in a huff. The prince thought for a moment. Then he went running after her.

'Georgiana,' he said in honeyed tones, 'Georgiana. I love you. Will you marry me?'

The princess turned round.

'*You* haven't gone down on one knee, I notice,' she said acidly.

Prince Blanziflor knelt down.

'PLEASE,' he begged.

The Princess Georgiana looked severely at him.

'You were *very* rude to me just now.'

'I'm sorry,' said the prince. 'I was still in a state of shock from the dragon and being in the cave so long and everything. And I think I was still a bit blinded by the light. *PLEASE*, Georgiana.'

The princess gave a gracious smile.

'All right then, I will.'

The prince cheered.

'But . . .' said the princess.

'Yes?'

'You can't just be king later on when we have our own kingdom. You have to take equal turns with me. A year each.'

'A year each it is,' agreed Blanziflor.

'And when we have royal babies you have to take turns at looking after them.'

'I'd like that,' said the prince. 'And *you*, Georgiana, will have to help me mow the palace lawns and clean the royal carriages.'

'But we've got fifteen gardeners,' objected the princess.

'Well, if we get poor, you'll have to.'

'All right,' said the princess. 'So it's all settled.'

'Yes.'

'By the way, Blanziflor . . .'

'Yes?'

'I love you too,' said the princess. 'And when I get home I'm having an octuple double strawberry-peanut - sausage - chocolate - crispy bacon - vanilla - peach-stardust icecream with treble flakes from my father's icecream machine. I really think I deserve it.'

'I think you do, too,' said the prince.

And he put his arm tenderly round her as they rode off together back to the palace.

Storm

by Kevin Crossley-Holland
Chosen by Sally Grindley
Editorial Director, Books for Children

'Seven swans a-swimming,' sang Annie, 'six geese a-laying . . .'

Annie was walking along the edge of the marsh, in no particular hurry because it was the first day of the Christmas holidays. After a while she began to practise clicking her fingers in time with the numbers. 'Three,' – CLICK! – 'three French hens, two,' – CLICK! – 'two turtle doves . . .'

Annie was used to being on her own. She was used to talking and singing to herself, and playing games like two-handed poohsticks and patience and solitaire. She really had no choice because her sister Willa was already grown up and married to Rod and expecting a baby and, anyhow, she lived fifty miles away.

Annie's parents, Mr and Mrs Carter, were rather old and not too well. Every day her mother complained that she felt as stiff as a whingeing hinge. 'It's that marsh,' she kept saying. 'The damp gets into my bones.' And since his stroke, her father was only able to walk with the help of two sticks. He had become quite mild and milky, like grain softened by mist.

Their cottage stood on its own at the edge of the great marsh, two miles away from the village of Waterslain. That marsh! Empty it looked and silent it seemed, but Annie knew better. She knew about the nests among the flags and rushes, she knew where to find the tunnels of the coypu and the dark pools teeming with shrimps and scooters. She knew the calls of the seabirds, the sucking sound of draining mud, the wind hissing in the sea lavender.

Every day in termtime Annie had to walk along this track at the edge of the marsh. She had to take off her shoes and socks to paddle across the ford of the river Rush, the little stream that bumbled all summer but burbled and bustled all winter when it was sometimes as much as twenty paces across. And then she hurried up the pot-holed lane to the crossroads where the school bus picked her up at twenty-to-nine and took her into Waterslain.

The only thing that Annie didn't like were the steely winter days when it began to grow dark before she came home from school. The marsh didn't seem such a friendly place then. The wind whined, seabirds screamed. At night, the boggarts and bogles and other marsh spirits showed their horrible faces. Once, Annie had heard the Shuck, the monster dog, coming up behind her and had only just got indoors in time.

Worst of all was the ghost who haunted the ford. Annie's mother said that he didn't mean to harm anyone, he just liked to play tricks on them and scare them. On one occasion Mrs Carter had dropped a basket of shopping into the water, and she complained the ghost had given her a push from behind. And the farmer, Mr Elkins, told Annie he had heard shouting and whinnying at the ford, but could see no man or horse to go with them. Annie always ran down the lane after school in winter so that she could get past the ford before it was completely dark.

'Two turtle doves,' sang Annie – CLICK! – 'and a partridge in a pear tree.'

'An-nie! An-nie!'

Annie turned round and saw her mother standing at the door of their cottage, waving.

'What?' she shouted. 'What is it?' But the wind

picked up her words and carried them off in the wrong direction. And why, wondered Annie, why have I got to go in when I was just going out?

'Lunch!' called her mother as soon as she heard Annie open the door and felt a tide of chill air washing round her ankles.

'Your sister's just been on the telephone. She's coming home tomorrow.'

'Willa!' cried Annie.

'You know the baby's due on Christmas Day?'

'Of course I know,' said Annie.

'Well, Willa says Rod can't get home now until early in the New Year.'

'Why not?' asked Annie.

'Just when she needs him,' said Annie's mother. 'Can you imagine? Thousands of miles away on the Indian Ocean.'

'I wouldn't like to marry a sailor,' said Annie.

'So she's coming home tomorrow,' her mother repeated, and then she smiled at Annie. 'She wants a bit of company.'

'What about the baby?' asked Annie.

'She'll have the baby in the cottage hospital,' said her mother. 'Doctor Grant has arranged that.'

'How long will she be in there?'

'Two days or seven days,' said Annie's mother. 'That's the rule.'

'Two I hope,' said Annie. 'Then it can sleep in my room.'

'It can sleep with Willa,' said her mother. 'Oh! That marsh. The damp gets into my bones.'

The next day, Annie and her mother crossed the ford and walked up to the crossroads and met Willa off the afternoon bus.

'What a journey!' said Willa.

'Two changes?' asked her mother.

'Three!' said Willa. 'This place is miles from anywhere.'

Annie said nothing. She had never thought of her home and the great marsh as miles from anywhere. To her, they were everywhere, everywhere that really mattered.

'Miles!' said Willa again. 'Hello, Annie!'

Annie felt quite shy as she kissed her sister. Perhaps Willa felt shy too. It always took them a few minutes before they got used to each other and found it easy to talk to each other again.

But once Annie and Willa began to talk, there was no stopping them.

They talked at breakfast and lunch and tea. They talked in between times. They talked as they walked along the marsh track and talked their way along the legs of the dyke that led out to the booming sea.

Willa told Annie what it felt like to be having a baby and Annie told Willa about school in Waterslain – the same school Willa had attended when she was a girl. Willa told Annie about town life. Annie told Willa the names of plants and birds.

'I never did learn them,' said Willa, 'and I always wish I had.'

When they came to the ford, Annie asked Willa about the ghost.

'He's here, all right. He's here,' said Willa. 'You know the story.'

'What story?' asked Annie.

'When he was alive – I mean when he had a body –

he used to own Mr Elkins' farm. That was in the days when there were highwaymen. Two of them ambushed him right there.'

Annie felt a cold finger slowly moving from the base of her spine up to her neck, and then spreading out across her shoulders.

'Where we're standing,' said Willa.

'What happened?' asked Annie.

'He wouldn't give them his money,' said Willa. 'He was that brave. So they killed him and his horse.'

'His horse!' cried Annie. 'That's horrible!' And at once she began to think of her lonely walks back from school – the dark January journeys lying in wait for her.

'So they got his money anyhow,' said Willa. 'That's what I've heard.'

'And the ghost?' said Annie.

'That goes up and down and around and pays out passers by,' said Willa. The sisters fell silent and stared at the flashing water.

On the third night after Willa came home there was a tremendous storm. Annie lay warm in her bed and listened to the wind going wild outside. It bumped and blundered against the walls of the cottage, it whistled between its salty lips and gnashed its sharp teeth.

As Annie dozed, she began to imagine she was not in bed but in a boat, rocking, quite safe, far out at sea. The sheets of rain lashing at her little window were small waves smacking at the bows, streaming down the boat's sides . . .

This was the night on which Willa's baby decided to be born. Just before midnight, it began to heave inside its mother like a buoy on surging water.

Everyone got up. Willa and Annie and their mother and even their father. All the lights were turned on again. The kettle began to sing.

'A cup of tea first,' said Annie's mother, looking pleased and shiny.

'You said Christmas,' protested Annie.

'You never can tell,' said her mother. 'Anyhow, early or late, storm or no storm, it's on its way. There's no stopping it now!'

'You could call it Storm,' said Mr Carter unexpectedly.

'That's not a name,' said Annie.

'Storm?' said Willa.

'Storm,' repeated Annie's mother. 'That's an old name in these parts.'

'Shall I ring the hospital?' said Willa. 'I know there's time but . . .'

'I'll ring while you get yourself packed and ready,' said her mother.

'Ask them to come for me in half-an-hour,' said Willa and, taking her tea with her, she went back upstairs to get ready.

When Annie's mother lifted the receiver, she first looked worried, and then she looked really alarmed.

'What's wrong?' said Mr Carter.

'Come and listen to this,' said Annie's mother.

Mr Carter dragged himself across the room and put an ear to the black receiver. Then he banged the telephone with the palm of his hand. He listened again. There was not a sound.

'Blast!' said Mr Carter. 'The lines are down.'

'What,' said Annie's mother, 'are we going to do?'

If anything, the storm was even fiercer now than it had been before. There was a howl of wind and a grating noise overhead, then outside the window a smash.

'Blast!' said Mr Carter. 'That's a tile gone.'

'What are we going to do, Bill?' repeated Annie's mother. 'We must get Doctor Grant. You can't walk and I must stay in case . . .'

'I'll go,' said Annie.

'No, no,' said her mother.

'I'm the only one who can,' Annie said. She had the strange feeling that it wasn't her but someone else speaking.

Mrs Carter frowned and shook her head.

'We can't do without a doctor,' said Annie. 'Willa can't.'

Annie's mother looked worried. 'It's the only way, Annie,' she said. 'We'll get you well wrapped up and you'll be all right. Go straight to Doctor Grant. Ask him to ring the hospital for an ambulance and then come at once himself.'

For once Annie took care over getting ready to go out. While her mother fussed round her and Willa sat very calm and upright on her bed, she put on her underclothes and then her track suit and then an old mackintosh over that. Her mother stuffed a hand-towel into one pocket and slipped a bar of chocolate into the other.

'I'll need my sou' wester,' said Annie. She picked up the hat from the floor, jammed it on and tied the lace under her chin.

'And your Wellingtons,' said her mother.

'What else?' said Annie. 'My scarf.'

'A torch,' said her mother. 'Though you know the way so well by now you could walk there backwards.'

'You're a real sport, Annie,' said Willa.

'It's only the ford I don't like,' said Annie. 'I don't mind the rest.'

'I know,' said Annie's mother. 'Make sure you dry yourself properly.'

'You'll soon get past it,' said Willa. Then she gasped, pressed the palms of her hands against her stomach, and breathed deeply. 'This baby,' she said. 'I think it's in a hurry.'

When Mrs Carter opened the cottage door, the wind snatched it out of her hands and slammed the door against the wall.

'Blast!' said Mr Carter. 'That's a rough old night!'

The four of them stood just inside the door, huddled together, staring out, getting used to the storm and the darkness.

There was a slice of moon well up in the sky. It seemed to be speeding behind grey lumpy clouds, running away from something that was chasing it. The Carters' little garden looked ashen and the marsh looked ashen and Mr Elkins' fields looked ashen.

They all heard it then: the sound of hooves, galloping.

'Blast!' said Mr Carter. 'Who can that be, then?'

'In this storm!' cried Annie's mother.

'At midnight,' said Mr Carter. Annie slipped one hand inside her mother's hand. The hooves drummed louder and louder, almost on top of them, and round the corner of the cottage galloped a horseman on a fine chestnut mare.

'Whoa!' shouted the rider when he saw Annie and her family standing at the cottage door.

'That's not Elkins, then,' said Mr Carter, hauling himself in front of his wife and daughters. 'That's not his horse.'

The horseman stopped just outside the pool of light streaming through the open door, and none of them recognised him. He was tall and unsmiling.

'That's a rough old night,' Mr Carter called out.

The horseman nodded and said not a word.

'Are you going into Waterslain?'

'Waterslain?' said the horseman. 'Not in particular.'

'Blast!' said Mr Carter in a thoughtful kind of way.

'I could go,' said the horseman in a dark voice, 'if there was a need.'

Then Annie's mother loosed her daughter's hand and stepped out into the storm and soon explained the need, and Mr Carter went out and asked the horseman his name. The wind gave a shriek and Annie was unable to catch his reply. 'So you see,' said Annie's mother, 'there's no time to be lost.'

'Come on up, Annie,' said the horseman.

'It's all right,' said Annie, shaking her head.

'I'll take you,' said the horseman.

'You'll be fine,' said Mrs Carter.

'I can walk,' insisted Annie.

But the horseman quickly bent down and put a hand under one of Annie's shoulders and swung her up onto the saddle in front of him as if she were as light as thistledown.

Annie's heart was beating fearfully. She bit hard on her lower lip.

Then the horseman raised one hand and spurred his horse. Mr and Mrs Carter stood and watched as Annie turned away the full white moon of her face and then she and the horseman were swallowed in the stormy darkness.

At first Annie said nothing and the horseman said nothing. But as the horse slowed to a trot and then began to wade across the ford, the horseman asked quietly, 'Are you afraid, Annie?'

'I am,' said Annie. 'I'm afraid for my sister and her baby,' she said. 'And I'm afraid of meeting the ghost.' She paused and then added in a sort of sob, 'I think I'd die if I met him tonight.'

At first the horseman didn't reply, and Annie thought it best not to say anything about being afraid of him as well, not knowing who he was. But then the rider suddenly reined in. 'Annie,' he said, 'your sister and her baby will be all right.'

'How do you know?' asked Annie.

'And you'll be all right,' said the horseman. 'There are ghosts and ghosts, Annie. Kind ghosts and unkind ghosts. You won't meet the ghost you fear between here and Waterslain.'

And so, step by step, Annie and the horseman slowly crossed the ford.

Now the chestnut mare quickened her stride again. It comforted Annie to feel the mare's warm neck and flanks, and after a while she leaned forward and buried her face in its mane.

With her eyes closed, Annie had the sense that she was not so much riding as flying – flying through the storm on a journey that might last forever.

He's a ghost himself, thought Annie. He's

bewitched us all and he's taking me away. He's taking me away into the always-darkness. No! No! That's wrong. No, he's my helper and we're going to the rescue of a maiden in distress.

When she sat up again, Annie felt quite dizzy. She shook her head and frowned. 'That's silly,' she told herself. 'You've been reading too many tales.'

And yet, wondered Annie, who is this rider? Where does he come from? And how did he happen to gallop right past our door just when we needed him? 'What's your name?' called Annie over her shoulder.

'What's that?' said the horseman. 'My name? Storm!'

'Storm!' cried Annie. 'That's even stranger.'

What a night it was! The salty wind was going round and round in circles, first whipping them forward, then holding them up, then barging them towards the hedge on one side of the lane or the deep ditch on the other. The horseman kept one arm round Annie and Annie held onto the horse. The rain flew straight at them, spiteful drops sharp as pins and needles.

Then Annie began to sway in the saddle. She thought she could bear it no longer – the furious gallop, the gallop of the storm, the storm of her own fears. What can I do, she thought. What can I do? What if I never get to Doctor Grant?

But the horseman only shouted and spurred his horse to go even faster. He seemed bent on going where he was going as quickly as he possibly could. Faster and faster! So that when Annie looked about her again, there she was! There she was in sleeping

Waterslain. The chestnut mare was sweating and blowing out big puffs of condensed air.

'Down Staithe Street,' gasped Annie. 'Doctor Grant.'

The horseman galloped straight up the middle of the village street. The horse's hooves clattered on the tarmac and Annie saw that several times they struck sparks from pieces of chert and flint. Then they turned into Staithe Street and 'Whoa!' shouted the horseman in his dark voice.

'Whoa!' And his mare at last slowed down to a trot.

'There!' said Annie, pointing to a gateway flanked by laurel bushes. 'We're there!'

Doctor Grant's lights were still on. His curtains were the colour of ripe peaches. And a lantern, swaying in his porch, threw a pool of soft shifting light over the flagstones and gravel outside the front door.

Annie started and stared as if she had never seen bright light before. In the gloom of the great storm, nothing had looked quite definite and many things looked frightening: the reaching arms of the tree, the fallen body of the milk churn, the gleam and flash of water. There was the danger, too, of meeting these chancy things that only come out at night – will-o'-the-wykes and bogles and boggarts and the black dog, Shuck . . . and worst of all there was the ghost. But now, in the clear light, there was no longer room for anything uncertain or ghostly.

Annie relaxed her grip on the horse and took a deep breath. And when she slowly let her breath out again, she felt as if she had been holding it in ever since she left home.

'So, Annie,' said the horseman, 'this is where I must leave you.'

'Come in!' cried Annie. 'I'm sure you can come in.'

'You must go your way and I mine,' said the horseman, shaking his head, and taking great care to stop his horse from putting so much as a hoof into the pool of light. 'Your sister and her baby will be all right.'

So Annie swung down out of the saddle and stood on the gravel, feeling rather shaky. She looked up at the man, still unsmiling and sitting so still.

'Thank you,' cried Annie. 'Thank you. I was so afraid.' She shook her head. 'I was afraid of meeting the ghost.'

'There was no fear of that,' said the horseman. 'Annie,' he said, 'I *am* the ghost.'

Annie drew in her breath with a sob. She raised her arms and for one second closed her eyes as tight as cockleshells.

When she opened them again there was nobody there, no horseman and no horse.

Dr Grant's lantern still creaked and swayed in the porch, and its light shone over the flagstones and gravel, but Storm and his chestnut mare, they had both completely vanished.

Harvey Angell (Chapter 6)
by Diana Hendry
Chosen by Sally Brummitt
Product Group Manager, Children's Books, W. H. Smith

Supper with Harvey Angell at the table was very different from any supper Harvey had known at 131 Ballantyre Road. To begin with, Harvey Angell was very complimentary about Aunt Agatha's cooking.

'What deliciously tender chicken,' he said, quickly eating the fragment on his plate. 'I'll have another helping of that if you don't mind, Miss Agatha.'

There was a hush at the table. Everyone waited for Aunt Agatha's eyebrows to arch and for her familiar speech about controlling the appetite. But it seemed Aunt Agatha didn't mind. She went over to the oven and fetched the pot. Mr Perkins, Miss Muggins, Miss Skivvy and Henry all stared in astonishment, their knives and forks poised in midair, as Aunt Agatha gave Harvey Angell a second – and really quite generous – portion of chicken.

'Well, if there're seconds going . . .' said Mr Perkins cheerfully.

'There aren't,' said Aunt Agatha, clamping the lid back on the pot. 'Mr Angell doesn't eat breakfast. Nor, if I might remark, does he have any excess weight about his person.'

Mr Perkins glowered. Harvey Angell leant across the table to Miss Muggins.

'Forgive me asking, Miss Muggins,' he said, giving her the irresistible 500 kilowatt beam, 'but was it you I heard singing in the room beneath mine this evening?'

Miss Muggins became very red and tearful. 'I'm most terribly sorry, Mr Angell,' she said, giving a frightened glance at Aunt Agatha. 'It was such a nice evening that I couldn't resist singing to myself. I was trying to do it as quietly as I could. I'm most sorry if I disturbed you. Most sorry indeed. I do assure you it won't happen again.'

'Nothing to be sorry about,' said Harvey Angell. 'I enjoyed listening.'

Miss Muggins was thoroughly flustered by this. 'Oh, how very kind,' she kept saying until Mr Perkins, still cross that he hadn't been allowed second helpings, slammed down his knife and fork saying, 'Fine words butter no parsnips.'

'I beg your pardon, Mr Perkins,' said Miss Muggins. 'We don't have any parsnips, do we?'

Mr Perkins groaned.

'Nothing makes a place more like home than a little music, a song or two,' continued Harvey Angell, 'and I see we have a piano over there.'

The cheek of this stranger was all too much for Mr Perkins. 'It's locked!' he shouted, pushing his chair away from the table, standing up and waving his pudding spoon at Harvey Angell. 'It's locked like everything else in this house. Locked up like the fridge at night. Locked up like the tea bags. Locked up like laughter, like love . . . like . . . like Hearts in Unkind Bosoms!' finished Mr Perkins and with something almost like a sob left the room.

'Oh dear,' said Miss Muggins, 'did he want parsnips that badly?'

'Mr Perkins is a poet,' said Aunt Agatha calmly. 'I'm afraid he's very moody and temperamental. I do apologise on his behalf, Mr Angell.'

'Mr Perkins works in the bank,' said Henry. (He'd been on Mr Perkins' side about the second helping.)

'No,' said Aunt Agatha. 'He only *pretends* to work in a bank. I've known it for years.'

'Anyway,' she continued, 'neglect and hunger are good for poets. They write much better poems without second helpings.'

'Well, you should know about the artistic temperament, I suppose,' said Harvey Angell. 'Being a musician yourself that is.' Henry say that Harvey Angell was giving Aunt Agatha the Full Beam. He waited for his aunt's anger, waited for the speech about music and moral fibres.

Instead Aunt Agatha flushed scarlet and suddenly looked very shy. 'However did you know?' she asked.

'He sniffed it out,' said Henry, making a wild guess.

'Henry, don't be silly,' snapped Aunt Agatha.

'You've got pianist's hands,' said Harvey Angell. Aunt Agatha promptly hid them under the table-cloth.

'People think that pianists have long slender fingers,' said Harvey Angell, 'but you only have to look at the hands of some famous pianists to know that's not true. I've seen photographs of Anton Rubinstein's hands – stumpy little fingers he had but a long stretchy thumb. And Frank Liszt, much the same.'

'Do show us your hands, Miss Agatha,' said Miss Skivvy and, reluctantly pleased, Aunt Agatha took her hands out from under the cloth and spread them out on the table. Everyone leaned forward to admire them. Aunt Agatha stretched her thumb out as far as it would go – which was at a right angle to her fingers. Everyone else tried to do the same and failed.

'Well, isn't this grand then,' said Harvey Angell. 'It

seems we've got one singer and one pianist. We can have a sing-song.'

There was a sudden silence. This is it, thought Henry, he's gone too far this time.

'The piano *is* locked, Mr Angell,' Miss Skivvy whispered as if she was saying 'the piano's dead,' as well it might be thought Henry, locked up and unplayed like that for years.

'Henry, the key is on the top shelf of the dresser,' said Aunt Agatha suddenly.

Henry fetched a stool and reached up for the key. He dusted it off on the back of his trousers.

'I'll just pop up for my flute, then I can join in,' said Harvey.

Henry looked to see if Aunt Agatha flinched at this clear infringement of the No Music rule, but she didn't. It was as if, Henry thought, Harvey Angell's Beam cast a kind of spell on Aunt Agatha. He thought of Ginger-Whiskers and his trombone. A pity he isn't here too, he thought, then we'd have a regular orchestra.

'What about you now, Miss Skivvy,' said Harvey Angell pausing at the door, 'any musical accomplishments?'

'Well, I can recite,' said Miss Skivvy. 'I know the *Forsaken Merman* off by heart.' Henry had never seen Miss Skivvy so excited except during their illicit tea-making sessions.

'Splendid!' said Harvey Angell, making for the stairs. 'I'll knock on Mr Perkins' door as I go up. Perhaps he'll read us one of his poems?'

It was a wonderful evening. Afterwards Henry tried

to think what had happened to Aunt Agatha and why, at the piano, she had seemed so different.

Something happened to the stiff winteriness of Aunt Agatha's body when she sat down at the piano. Maybe your Aunt Agatha needs oiling, Harvey Angell had said. Well that was it. The music worked like oil which got inside Aunt Agatha and oiled all her bones and joints. Aunt Agatha swayed and bent to the music and sometimes even joined in the singing with Miss Muggins.

Henry had expected Miss Muggins to have a high, thin little voice – a voice that matched her size. But no! Miss Muggins had a powerfully deep voice. She sang *Land of Hope and Glory* and another song called *The Old Folks at Home* which made Miss Skivvy cry.

Mr Perkins had been persuaded to come downstairs by Harvey Angell but he still looked very cross.

'Some people have only been here five minutes and then take over the place,' he said. 'They are given quite unwarranted privileges. For myself,' said Mr Perkins, 'I do not like people who go sniffing about the place,' and he looked very pointedly at Harvey Angell.

That gave Henry a shock. In the enjoyment of the evening he had temporarily forgotten his doubts about Harvey Angell. Doubts which, it seemed, were shared by Mr Perkins.

'Mr Perkins, you're being very foolish,' said Aunt Agatha. 'You're only jealous. Have you brought a poem down?'

(Poor Mr Perkins, thought Henry, he can't charm Aunt Agatha with a Beam). But Mr Perkins *did* have a poem. It was pages and pages long. Henry couldn't understand a word of it but it seemed to be about love.

Everyone applauded at the end except for Aunt Agatha who said, 'Reeee-asonable, Mr Perkins, but you could cut the third verse and the seventh and the tenth and it would be much better.'

Mr Perkins sat down and sulked.

'Well, I thought that was very fine,' said Harvey Angell. 'Poets are very like electricians. We're on the same circuit, you could say. Exploring the Energy Fields. There was once a very fine poet called William Blake who said 'Energy is Eternal Delight'."

'I don't know what you're talking about,' said Mr Perkins crossly. 'Poets are nothing like electricians. Nothing at all.'

But Harvey Angell only laughed at this and then it was Miss Skivvy's turn to give her recitation.

Henry liked Miss Skivvy's poem better than Mr Perkins' poem even though it was just as long and he fell asleep in the middle of it.

Miss Skivvy's poem was about a merman and his children calling for a lost mother. It was a roundabout sort of poem with lines that kept on repeating themselves like the call of the children. In Henry's sleepy brain the lines went round and round too, so that he seemed to be joining in the sadness of the forsaken merman when he sang,

> Children's voices should be dear
> (Call once more) to a mother's ear;
> Children's voices wild with pain –
> Surely she will come again!
> Call her once and come away;

This way, this way!
'Mother dear, we cannot stay!
The wild white horses foam and fret.'
Margaret! Margaret!

Come, dear children, come away down;
Call no more!
One last look at the white-wall'd town,
And the little grey church on the
    windy shore;
Then come down!
She will not come though you call all day;
Come away, come away!

'A very sad poem,' said Harvey Angell when Miss
Skivvy, wiping her eyes because she had been so
moved by her own performance, had finished.

'Even though I'm very old,' said Miss Skivvy, 'I
often miss my mother.'

'I know the feeling,' said Harvey Angell. 'A mother
lost is a paradise lost. At least we think it's lost,
though it's there, on the circuit, all the time.'

(Anyone would think, thought Henry, that
mothers were being lost all over the place, that they
were as easily lost as handkerchiefs or homework.)

'All this about circuits, all this electrical jargon,'
said Mr Perkins irritably, 'I've had enough of it!'

'I think you should give us a tune, Mr Angell,' said
Miss Muggins. 'Something to cheer us all up.'

So Harvey Angell played his flute and Henry felt
very wide awake then because it was a very happy
tune so that even Mr Perkins was soon tapping his
feet to the rhythm.

Harvey Angell walked about as he played. Henry thought of how, when it was very hot in late summer, Aunt Agatha walked about the kitchen with her Death Spray, killing flies and wasps. Harvey Angell walked about with his flute in much the same way, only he was blowing music – Life Spray – into every corner.

After this Harvey Angell said he must go to bed for he had to be up early in the morning for work and everyone else discovered how late it was too.

Aunt Agatha was about to lock the piano up again when Henry said, 'Leave it open, Aunt Agatha. Please.' And Aunt Agatha gave him an odd kind of look and said, 'Well, all right Henry.'

Then to his astonishment she opened the window onto the back garden and threw the key away.

It had, he thought as he undressed for bed, been a whole day of surprises. From the moment Harvey Angell had arrived things had begun to change. And the people in the house had changed too. Or maybe, thought Henry, it wasn't that they had changed but just that he had learnt more about them. Miss Muggins, for instance, and her singing; Mr Perkins and his poems; Aunt Agatha and her mother who had upped and offed; and Great-Grandma Ellie who once upon a time had seemed as unreal as a person in a book and who now, even though she was dead, seemed very real indeed.

A little parade of woodlice crossed Henry's floor. Henry knelt down to look at them. He was fond of woodlice. They looked like armoured trucks. They all looked exactly alike – although some were bigger than others – but probably, if you got to know them, they all had very different characters. 'Do you sing, Mr Woodlouse?' Henry asked the woodlouse leader, 'or do you play the flute?' Then he laughed at himself and got into bed.

The dark bushing shrub outside his window rustled against the pane. It seemed to Henry that the shrub and the darkness had caught the echo of Miss Skivvy's poem and as he began to doze off, the lines of the poem went round and round in Henry's head:

She will not come though you call all day;
Come away, come away!

And then Henry was going down, down, down into the under-the-sea world of sleep.

Suddenly – at least it seemed sudden, but it must have been two or three hours later – he was wide awake again. There were footsteps on the stairs.

The stairs of 131 Ballantyre Road were very creaky. During Mr Murgatroyd's stay in the attic, Henry (sometimes wanting to creep up there to share a crust of Granary, Harvester or Bloomer) had learnt how to go up and down them avoiding the creaks.

Whoever was out there now hadn't. Henry knew the footsteps of everyone in the house, even the very light ones of Miss Muggins.

Henry slid out of bed and very quietly opened his door. Very quietly – avoiding the creaks – he crept halfway up the stairs.

In the moonlight that shone through the landing window Henry saw him, Harvey Angell, peering into the linen cupboard at the top of the stairs and – yes –

sniffing!

Sniffing about! An occupation that surely belonged to thieves, criminals and kidnappers! What was Harvey Angell doing in the middle of the night sniffing about in the airing cupboard? Sniffing out treasure maybe? Did Aunt Agatha have any gold and silver? Had Great-Grandma Ellie a treasure horde? Had it all been locked up, like the piano, like – what was it Mr Perkins had said? Like Hearts in Unkind Bosoms. Gold and silver locked up in a chest somewhere?

Henry wondered if he should cough loudly or switch on the light and say casually, 'Hello there, Mr Angell. Looking for something? Can I help you?'

But the stairs and the landing with the moonlight shining down in the sleeping house seemed suddenly spooky. And what did he know about Harvey Angell? Really know? What was that song he'd sung while unpacking his Kit?

> Watts and volts,
> Watts and volts,
> Better by far
> than thunderbolts!

If he disturbed Harvey Angell now, mid-sniff as it were, he might very well turn round and throw a few watts and volts at Henry and Henry would be frizzled and fried on the instant.

He tiptoed back to bed and huddled under the blankets. Although it was a warm night, he felt The Shiver again.

But I *will* find out about him, Henry vowed to

himself. I'll find out exactly what he does with that Connecting Kit of his and – and this seemed a brain wave – I'll follow him one morning to the Energy Fields.

And with this thought Henry fell asleep. He dreamt that Harvey Angell had gone down to visit the merman and his children and was fitting their underwater palace with electric lights. The Forsaken Merman was very keen to have an electric kettle because he wanted to make tea. Tea was very comforting the merman said. So Harvey Angell fitted an electric kettle with a piece of sea-weed for the lead and the merman boiled it. But when the kettle boiled, the sea boiled too and then Aunt Agatha appeared like some ancient, sea-wrinkled queen and said he wasn't to boil that kettle ever again. It was a waste of electricity.

The Guard Dog
by Dick King-Smith
Chosen by Stephanie Nettell
Author and Children's Books Reviewer,
The Guardian (1978-1992)

There were six puppies in the window of the pet shop. People who knew about dogs would have easily recognised their breeds. There was a Labrador, a springer spaniel, an Old English bobtail, a poodle and a pug.

But even the most expert dog-fancier couldn't have put a name to the sixth one. In fact most of those who stopped to look in the pet-shop window either didn't notice it (because it was so extremely small), or thought it was a rough-haired guinea-pig (which it resembled in size and shape) that had got into the wrong pen.

'What on earth is that?' the rest had said to one another when the sixth puppy was first put in with them. 'Looks like something the cat dragged in!' And they sniggered amongst themselves.

'I say!' said the Old English bobtail puppy loudly. 'What are you?'

The newcomer wagged a tail the length of a pencil-stub. 'I'm a dog,' it said in an extremely small voice.

The pug snorted.

'You could have fooled me,' said the poodle.

'Do you mean,' said the Labrador, 'you're a dog, as opposed to a bitch?'

'Well, yes.'

'But what sort of dog?' asked the springer spaniel.

'How d'you mean, what sort?'

The pug snorted again, and then they all started barking questions.

'What breed are you?'

'What variety of dog?'

'Why are you so small?'

'Why are you so hairy?'

'Are you registered with the Kennel Club?'

'How many Champions have you in your pedigree?'

'Pedigree?' said the sixth puppy. 'What's a pedigree?'

There was a stunned silence, broken at last by a positive volley of snorts.

'Pshaw!' said the pug. 'He's a mongrel!'

At that they all turned their backs and began talking among themselves.

'I say!' said the Labrador. 'D'you know what I'm going to be when I grow up?'

'A gun dog, I bet,' said the springer spaniel, 'like me. I'm going to be a gun dog and go out with my master and bring back the pheasants he shoots.'

'No,' said the Labrador, 'as a matter of fact I'm not. I'm going to be a guide dog for the blind. A much more worthwhile job.'

'No more worthwhile than mine,' said the Old English bobtail. 'I'm going to work sheep. I'll be galloping about all over the countryside . . .'

'. . . getting filthy dirty,' interrupted the poodle, 'while I'm having my coat shampooed and specially trimmed and clipped, and a silk ribbon tied in my topknot. I'm going to be a show dog and win masses of prizes.'

The pug snorted.

'What about you?' barked the others. 'You haven't said what you're going to be when you grow up.'

'I am going to be a lap-dog,' said the pug loftily. 'I shall be thoroughly spoiled and eat nothing but chicken and steak, and the only exercise I shall take will be to walk to my food-dish. Pshaw!'

'What about me?' said that extremely small voice. 'You haven't asked me what I'm going to be when I grow up.'

The Labrador yawned. 'Oh, all right,' it said. 'Tell us if you must.'

'I,' said the sixth puppy proudly, 'am going to be a guard dog.'

At this the others began to roll helplessly about, yapping and yelping and snorting with glee.

'A guard dog!' they cried.

'Mind your ankles, burglars!'

'He's not tall enough to reach their ankles!'

'If he did, those little teeth would only tickle them!'

'Perhaps his bark is worse than his bite!'

'It is!' said the sixth puppy. 'Listen!'

Then out of his hairy little mouth came the most awful noise you can possibly imagine. It was a loud noise, a very, very loud noise for such a tiny animal, but its volume was nothing like as awful as the tone of it.

Think of these sounds: chalk scraping on a blackboard, a wet finger squeaking on a window-pane, a hacksaw cutting through metal, rusty door-hinges creaking, an angry baby screaming, and throw in the horrible bubbly sound of someone with a really nasty cough. Mix them all up together and there you have the noise that the sixth puppy made.

It was a dreadful noise, a revolting disgusting jarring vulgar noise, and it set all the creatures in the pet shop fluttering and scuttering about in panic. As for the other puppies, they bunched together as far away as they could get, their hackles raised, their lips wrinkled in loathing.

82

At last, after what seemed an age, the sixth puppy stopped. Head on one side, he wagged his pencil-stub tail.

'You see,' he said happily in his usual extremely small voice. 'I can make quite a rumpus when I really try.'

'Nobody will buy him,' said the other puppies later. 'That's for sure.'

'What a racket!' said the sheep-dog.

'It made me feel quite ill!' said the gun dog.

'A really common noise!' said the guide dog.

'Made by a really common animal!' said the show dog.

'Phsaw!' said the lap-dog.

They all stared balefully at the guard dog.

'The sooner he's sold, the better,' they said.

And that afternoon, he was.

Into the pet shop walked a tall lady with a face that looked as though it had a bad smell under its nose, and a small fat girl.

'I am looking for a puppy,' said the lady to the shopkeeper, 'for my daughter. I know nothing about dogs. Which of these would you recommend?'

All the puppies lolloped forward to the inner wire of the pen, whining and wagging and generally looking as irresistible as puppies do.

All, that is, except the guard dog. He sat alone, small and silent. He was not exactly sulking – that was not in his nature – but he still felt very hurt.

'Nobody will buy him. That's for sure,' they had said.

He resigned himself to life in a pet shop.

The shopkeeper was busy explaining the various virtues of the five pedigree puppies when the fat child, who was standing sucking her thumb, took it out with a plop. She pointed at the guard dog.

'Want that one,' she said.

'Oh, that's just a mongrel puppy, dear,' said the shopkeeper. 'I expect Mummy would prefer . . .'

'Want that one.'

'But darling . . .'

The small fat girl stamped her small fat foot. She frowned horribly. She hunched her shoulders. With a movement that was as sudden as it was decisive, she jammed her thumb back in her small fat mouth.

'She wants that one,' said her mother.

By the end of that day, the guard dog was feeling pretty pleased with life. To be sure, there were things about his new owners that he did not quite understand. It seemed, for example, that simple pleasures like chewing carpets and the bottom edges of curtains drove the lady into what he considered a quite unreasonable rage, and as for the child, she was temperamental, he thought, to say the least.

Though at first she had seemed willing to play with him, she soon began to complain that his teeth were too sharp or his claws too scratchy or his tongue too slobbery, and had made a ridiculous fuss over a doll which had sported a fine head of hair and was now bald.

Strange creatures, he thought that night when at last all was quiet, but I musn't grumble. I'm warm and well-fed and this seems a very fine house for a guard dog to guard. Which reminds me – it's time I was off on my rounds. Ears cocked, nose a-quiver, he pattered off on a tour of the downstairs rooms.

His patrol over, he settled down in a basket in the kitchen. There was plain evidence that he had done his duty. In the centre of the drawing-room, for example, there was a fine white fleecy rug, and in the centre of the rug was a bright yellow pool. In other rooms there were other offerings.

Comfortable now, the guard dog closed his extremely small eyes. It had been a tiring day, and he was just drifting off to sleep when suddenly, outside the kitchen door, he heard a stealthy sound!

He leaped to his feet.

Afterwards they could not understand why their cat would never again enter the house, but lived, timidly, in the garden shed. They did not know that its nerves had been shattered by the simple act of pressing against the cat-flap, something it had done every day of its life. This had resulted instantly in a noise that sounded to its horrifed ears like a number of cats being scrunched up in a giant mincer. Upstairs, the fat child woke screaming, and soon her mother came rushing down those stairs and stepped in something unusual at the bottom.

Even then the guard dog might still have had a house to guard (for it was difficult for them to believe that so little a creature was capable of making so ghastly a noise), if only he had kept his mouth shut next morning. But he stuck to his task, challenging everything that seemed to him a threat to the territory which it was his duty to protect.

Quite early, at the sound of whistling and the chink of bottles outside the door, he woke his owners once more. And no sooner had they taken the milk in than the postman knocked, and they actually saw the guard dog in action.

Happily unaware of the effect of his voice upon the human ear, and mindful only of his role – to give warning of the approach of strangers – the guard dog kept it up all morning. The cleaning woman (who found a great deal of cleaning to do), a door-to-door salesman, the electricity man come to read the meter, and a Jehovah's Witness were each in turn greeted by the dreadful medley of sounds that emerged, full blast, from the guard dog's tiny throat. Last came a collector for the RSPCA, the rattle of whose tin inspired the guard dog to his loudest, longest and most furious outburst.

'RSPCA?' screamed his distracted owner. 'What about a society for the prevention of cruelty to people?' And by mid-day, as she unscrewed the aspirin bottle, she said to her daughter, 'I'm sorry, darling, but I cannot stand that row a moment longer. It'll have to go. Will you be very upset?'

The small fat girl, her eyes fixed malevolently upon the guard dog, did not even bother to remove her thumb from her mouth. She merely shook her head, violently.

That afternoon the guard dog found himself, to his surprise, in a very different kind of home, the Dogs' Home. He could not make out what had gone wrong. What were guard dogs meant to do if not guard? He had only done his duty, but all he had so far received had been angry looks and angry words before finally they bundled him into their car, and drove him to a strange place full of strange dogs and left him.

From the kennel he had been given, Number 25, he looked around him. There was every sort of dog in the kennel block, young and old, handsome and ugly, large and small (though none remotely as small as he). Why were they all there?

'Why are we all here?' he asked the dog directly opposite him, a sad-looking animal with long droopy ears and a long droopy face.

'Because,' said the dog dolefully, 'we are all failures.'

I don't get it, thought the guard dog. My job is to give warning of the approach of strangers. I've never yet failed in that.

'I don't think I'm a failure,' he said.

'Well, you're certainly not a success,' said the long-faced dog, 'or you wouldn't be here. All of us are here because our owners couldn't stand us any longer.'

'But we'll get new owners, won't we?'

'Possibly. It depends.'

'Depends on what?'

'On whether you take someone's fancy. You just have to do whatever you're best at. Me, I'm best at looking sad. Some people like that.'

In the days that followed, many people in search of a suitable pet came to inspect the twenty or so current inmates of the Dogs' Home; and when they came to the end of the range of kennels and found the smallest inhabitant, they would without exception break into smiles at the sight of so charming a little scrap.

Without exception, however, they were treated to the dreadful spectacle of the guard dog doing what he was best at.

And without exception the smiles vanished, to be replaced by looks of horror, as they turned away with their hands clapped to their ears.

By the time the guard dog had been in the Dogs' Home for a week, most of the animals had gone happily (or in the case of the long-faced dog, sadly) away with new owners, and there were newcomers in most of the kennels. By the thirteenth day, there was only one dog left of those who had been there when he was admitted. This was his next-door neighbour, an old and rather smelly terrier.

The guard dog's attempts to make conversation with it had always thus far been met with a surly growl, so that he was quite surprised when he was suddenly addressed.

'You bin in 'ere thirteen days, littlun, ain't you?' said the terrier.

'Oh,' said the guard dog, 'have I?'

'Ar. You come in day after I. 'Tis my fourteenth day.'

'Oh well,' said the guard dog, 'try not to worry. I'm sure you'll soon be gone.'

'Ar,' said the terrier. 'I shall. Today.'

'But how can you know that? How can you know that someone's going to take you away today?'

'Fourteen days is the limit, littleun. They don't keep you no longer than that.'

'Why, what do they do with you then?'

'Ain't nobody told you?'

'No.'

'Ar well,' said the old terrier. ''Tis all right for us old uns, 'tis time to go. I shan't be sorry. You don't feel nothing, they do say. But 'tis a shame for a nipper like you.'

'I don't understand,' said the guard dog. 'What are you trying to tell me?' But though he kept on asking, the old dog only growled at him, and then lay silent, staring blankly out of its kennel. Later, a man in a white coat came and led it gently away.

'Oh thanks,' said the manager of the Dogs' Home, when one of his kennelmaids brought in his cup of coffee at eleven o'clock next morning. He looked up from his record book.

'Shame about that little titchy one in Number 25,' he said.

'You don't mean . . .?' said the kennelmaid.

''Fraid so. If things had been slack we could have kept him longer, but the way dogs are pouring in, we must keep to the two-week rule. He's one for the vet today.'

'Oh dear,' said the kennelmaid. 'He's such a lovely little fellow. Dozens of people fell for him, until . . .'

'. . . until he opened his mouth,' said the manager. 'I know. It's a pity, but you can't blame them. In all my long experience of every sort of dog, I've never come across one with such a dreadful voice. Nobody could possibly live with that – though talk about burglar alarms, any burglar would run a mile if he heard that hullabaloo. And you wouldn't need to dial 999, they'd hear it at the nearest police station, easy.'

The guard dog ate a hearty breakfast, and was a little surprised, when the kennelmaid came to clean out his run, at the fuss she made of him. She cuddled and stroked and kissed him as if she would never see him again.

Then he remembered what the smelly old terrier had said. This is my fourteenth day, he thought. Great! Someone will pick me out today!

He sat, waiting for the time when the public were admitted, determined that today of all days he would leave no one in any doubt as to the quality of his greatest asset. Other guard dogs, he supposed, might act in other ways, by looking large and fierce (which he could not), or by leaping up and planting their feet on the shoulders of burglars and suchlike and knocking them flat (which he most certainly could not). He had only his voice, and when the door to the kennel block opened he let rip, *fortississimo*.

No one even got to smiling at him that morning. Everybody kept as far away as possible from the dreadful sounds issuing from Number 25, and concentrated upon the other inmates. The guard dog was left strictly alone.

When at last the batch of would-be owners had left, some with new companions, some empty-handed, all mightily relieved to reach the comparative peace and quiet of the busy roaring street outside, the guard dog sat silent once more. There was a puzzled look on his extremely small hairy face.

Can't understand it, he thought, nobody seems to want a decent guard dog. But if fourteen days was the limit, then they'd jolly well have to find him somewhere to go today. Perhaps the man in the white coat would take him too – he seemed a nice sort of chap.

He watched the door to the kennel block.

It was not the man in the white coat who came in but the kennelmaid, and a white-haired man who walked with a stick with a rubber tip.

'Would you like me to come round with you?' the kennelmaid said, but he did not answer, so she went away and left him alone.

The old man walked slowly along the row of kennels, looking into each carefully with sharp blue eyes. At last he came to Number 25.

Outside the door, the kennelmaid stood listening, her fingers tightly crossed. But then she heard the fearful noise start up and shook her head sadly. She went back into the kennel block to find the old man squatting on his heels. There was a grin on his face as he looked, apparently totally unmoved, at the howling bawling yowling squalling guard dog. He levered himself to his feet.

'I'll have this little fellow,' he said firmly. 'He's the boy for me.'

'Oh good!' cried the kennelmaid. 'He's lovely, don't you think?' But the old man did not answer. He did not reply either, later, when he had paid for the guard dog and the kennelmaid said, 'Would you like a box to carry him in?' And in answer to the manager's question, 'What are you going to call him?' he only said, 'Good afternoon.'

Light suddenly dawned on the manager of the Dogs' Home. He stood directly in front of the guard dog's new owner so as to be sure of catching his eye, and said deliberately, in a normal tone, 'That's some dog you've got there. The worst voice in the world!'

The old man put his hand up to his ear. 'Sorry?' he said. 'Didn't catch that. I'm as deaf as a post and I can't be bothered with those hearing-aid things, never been able to get on with them. What did you say?'

'That's some dog you've got there. The best choice in the world!' said the manager very loudly.

The white-haired old man only smiled, leaning on his stick with one hand and cradling his purchase in the other.

The manager shouted as loud as he could, 'He's a dear little chappie!'

'See that he's really happy?' said the old man. 'Of course I will, you needn't worry about that. We'll be as happy as two peas in a pod.' He fondled the puppy's extremely small hairy ears. 'Funny,' he said, 'I fell for him though he wasn't actually what I was looking for. I live all on my own, you see, so really it would have been more sensible to get a guard dog.'

Burper and the Magic Lamp
by Robert Leeson
Chosen by Sonia Benster
Proprietor, Children's Bookshop, Huddersfield, Yorkshire

This is the story of Roderick. That is what his parents called him. Don't ask me why. Parents do funny things when they choose names for their children.

But in class, they call him Burper.

Not to his face of course. Oh no.

They called him Burper for a very good reason. He was always burping. He didn't do it after school dinner, like anybody might – just once at the beginning of the afternoon. He would do it at break time. He would do it in PE. He'd do it in English. He'd even do it in Assembly.

Miss would look up, over her glasses and say, 'Which ill-mannered person did that?'

Everybody knew who'd done it. But they didn't say. Not on your nelly. Miss probably knew, but she couldn't be sure. After all if someone has just burped how can you prove it? Do you take a tape recording and hold an identity parade?

So Roderick got away with it. He got away with most things. He was bigger than anyone in the class. He was bigger than anyone in the school. Whichever way you looked at him he was bigger. He was bigger this way and he was bigger that way.

Now some people get fat because they are unhappy and some people get fat because there's something wrong with their body.

There were two things wrong with Burper. He ate too much and he didn't get any exercise. His parents thought he was marvellous and they waited on him at home. And people waited on him at school. He made them. Anything Burper had to do, someone else did it for him. And to be honest, Burper was a pig. A big, fat, pig.

He always got his way. He always got what he wanted. And the more he got, the more he wanted.

But what he wanted most of all, he couldn't have.

Poor old Burper.

Well, not really.

What happened was that Burper fell in love.

It was a disaster.

He fell disastrously in love.

A new girl came to our school. She was called Djamila. She was very small. She was the smallest in the class. She had dark brown eyes with long eyelashes and wore her hair in two plaits down her back.

When she started in the class everyone held their breath.

They all knew what was going to happen. That big onk Burper was going to go up behind her and pull those plaits. Or maybe he was going to tie them together. Or tie her to the railings in the school yard by them. It wasn't fair. Burper was the biggest in the class, but he always picked on the smallest. Funny, isn't it?

Some of the lads and some of the girls wondered what they should do about it. Djamila was so small and thin, it seemed rotten to let Godzilla (or rather Burper) get his paws on her. The trouble was though, not what you *should* do about it, but what you *could* do about it.

The first day Djamila came to school it was raining. No one could go out in the yard. Miss was out of the classroom somewhere. Suddenly there was Burper creeping up behind Djamila. He was actually creeping. Imagine an elephant on tiptoe. That was it.

Everyone held their breath and waited.

Just as Burper got a foot away from Djamila, she turned round so quickly, one of her plaits hit him in the eye. He jumped like a scalded cat (a scalded elephant) and Djamila said, 'Hello fat boy. What's your name?'

She said it so sweetly that Burper didn't know what to do with himself. He stuttered. He actually stuttered.

From the back of the class someone whispered (loud enough for her to hear, but not loud enough for him to tell who had spoken).

'His name's Burper.'

'Oh,' said Djamila. 'Is that your first name or your second name.'

Burper burst out, 'Roderick.'

'Oh, is that Roderick Burper or Burper Roderick? I'm not used to which way round names go.'

The whole class began to laugh.

She went on. Some people thought she was putting Burper on. But she wasn't. Her face was quite straight.

'Can I call you Burper?'

The class howled and the place was in an uproar when in walked Miss.

'Ha, hm,' she said in that way of hers. 'Do you mind?'

The class went quiet. Miss looked at Burper and pointed to his seat. Burper went quietly.

Miss said, 'Djamila is starting with us today. I hope you'll all be friends with her.'

Djamila put her hand up.

'I've made one friend already, Miss. Burper.'

People all round the class started to choke. Miss tried to keep a straight face.

'Strictly speaking, Djamila, he is called Roderick.'

'Oh,' Djamila looked a bit confused now. 'I thought friends called him Burper.'

The class looked round at Burper to see how he was taking it. But it was weird. He wasn't screwing his face up like he does when he's deciding whether to twist somebody's arm off, or pull their hair till their eyes water. He sat there with a great, daft smile on his face.

It took Miss at least ten minutes to get the class settled down. Everybody knew, though, that something rather special had happened. They didn't know it was only just starting.

That lunchtime two lads who chanced their arm and called Roderick Burper just for fun, got minced. That hadn't changed. But the same day, when school finished, Djamila walked out of class and waved to him and called, 'See you tomorrow, Burper.'

And he went all mushy and said, 'Err-gghhh.'

Next day, and all the week, and all the next week, Burper could be seen hanging around Djamila. She had lots of friends, pretty quickly. She was that sort of girl. And after that first day, of course, she was a kind of heroine. But after the first few days, she didn't really pay much attention to Burper. The fact was, Burper wasn't really brilliant as company. His conversation was a bit limited. It was 'Gimme that,' or 'I'll thump you,' or 'You wait till break.'

And that didn't go down with Djamila. But he would hang about with her crowd, sometimes standing behind her. He wasn't planning to tie her plaits together either. He just stood there and breathed.

Sometimes she'd turn round and say, 'Hello, Burper.'

And he would answer, 'Errgghh.'

Or sometimes she would say, when he was breathing more heavily than usual, 'Please don't do that, Burper. You're giving me goose pimples.'

And then one day, when he was standing too close, she even lost her patience with him and said, 'Do leave it, Burper.'

The crowd round waited for Burper to fly into a rage. But he didn't, he just looked like an elephant whose bun ration has been stopped, and crawled back to his seat. That lunch-time he thought some of the lads were laughing at him (he was right). So he duffed them up, and felt a bit better. But towards the end of the afternoon he started looking miserable again.

'Is there something wrong, Roderick?' asked Miss. 'Perhaps you'd better go and see nurse.'

The class started laughing. But outside in the yard, nobody got clobbered. Burper just went slowly and sadly home.

It was just about then that the class started to make plans for the Christmas show. Since they were top class, they got to put on the Christmas play. And Miss had a smashing idea. She came into class one morning with a parcel which she unwrapped.

She held up an old metal thing, a bit like an old boot with a curly end.

'Can anyone guess what this is?' she asked.

'Do you really want us to, Miss?' asked one very

witty chap at the back.

'I want you to be sensible,' said Miss raising her eyebrows.

Then Djamila spoke.

'It's an old lamp, Miss. Like people used to use sometime at home, in days gone by. You put oil in it, and there's a little light at the end.'

'I thought you'd recognise it, Djamila. Right. It's an old lamp. My uncle brought it home from Baghdad. And guess what play we're going to put on.

'Let's get lit up,' suggested someone.

'This is a serious question,' said Miss in her 'that's enough' voice.

'*Aladdin*,' shouted several. And of course it was. And no one was surprised when she chose Djamila to be the Princess. It was obvious.

'Now, we have to choose Aladdin.'

Before anyone could move, Burper had his hand up. So one or two other lads who had thought of volunteering suddenly changed their minds. Miss kept a straight face, but slowly shook her head.

'Roderick. No. I'm afraid you do not look the part.'

She said it in a kindly way. But everybody knew what she meant. So did he.

Some smart alec at the back whispered, 'How about Widow Twankie? He'd look great in drag.'

There was a hush. But Burper didn't even turn round. At the end of the day, he was seen arguing with Miss by her desk. And she was shaking her head. He was getting desperate. But she would not give in. And Miss was one person in the class he couldn't lean on (apart from Djamila, that is).

Next morning there was a bit of a panic. Miss had

discovered the lamp was missing. The most important prop for the Panto had gone. There was a big to-do. In the end Miss said, 'If that lamp is not back on my desk by tomorrow morning, then no Panto. And the whole school will know – and your parents – why there's no Panto.'

One or two (well about twenty-five to be exact) were pretty sure who had nicked the old lamp. Yes, no prizes. It was Burper. He'd had away with it and hidden it round the back where the dustbins are. He couldn't make up mind what to do with it. He was better at thumping than thinking. Should he stick it right down inside one of the bins, then the rubbish vans would take it away and that would fix the Panto for good and all? Or should he 'find it' and make himself the hero of the day – and perhaps the hero of the panto? But Burper wasn't so stupid. He had his doubts about what Miss would do. She might blame him for taking it. And that wouldn't be fair, would it?

So that break-time it was raining again. While the class was indoors, Burper sneaking out to the toilets. Or he pretended to and went round to the rubbish bins instead. There were four of them, about six foot high, and he could hide behind them. He found the lamp where he had put it under one of the hoppers and held it up. It was covered in dirt though. He couldn't take it back like that could he? Without thinking he rubbed it on his sleeve?

Ka-bang.

Right in front of him was a bloke. A huge bloke. He made Burper look like Peter Pan. He was as big as a door, broad and dressed like Ali Baba. His hands were folded and he had a deep, deep voice.

'What is thy will, O Master?'

Burper, who had been crouching down, sat back in a puddle.

'Blimey,' he said. He was overcome.

'I am the slave of the lamp. Whatever you wish shall be yours.'

Burper recovered his wits.

'Hey, mister. I want to be Aladdin in the Pantomime.'

The genie shook his head.

'I do not understand. Alah-el-Din is no longer in the land of the living. He has been taken into Paradise.'

Burper bit his lip. This was going to be dodgy. Then he had a brainwave.

He pointed to himself and said, 'I, Roderick, am too fat.'

The genie looked him over, smiled and said, 'That is right. Ho-Ho.'

Burper didn't like that, but time was slipping away.

'I-want-to-lose-weight,' he said slowly.

A look of understanding came onto the genie's face. 'Aha. Lose weight.'

The genie waved his hand, and vanished into the lamp.

Burper looked at himself. And waited. And looked at himself again. There was no difference. He bent down and picked up the lamp. Either this thing didn't work or the genie had got it wrong.

But as he bent down, the ground seemed to go farther away from him. No, it wasn't the ground which was going farther away. He was going farther away from the ground. He was rising up in the air.

His feet were off the ground. He struggled and kicked out with his legs, but it made no difference. He was up as high as the top of the hoppers now, and his struggles didn't bring him down to earth. They just made him move along six feet off the ground. He was like a balloon, light as a feather. Slowly it came into his brain what had happened.

He'd 'lost weight'. But he hadn't got thinner. He was sailing along now. The rain had stopped and there was a slight breeze. Like a plump airship he was gliding towards the school. He was going to go 'splat' on the wall.

In a panic he used his right leg like a rudder. At the last moment he changed course and hung there just outside the window. Inside the class there was pandemonium as they saw Burper suspended in mid-air outside the glass, holding the lamp in front of him.

'It's a plane,' they shouted. 'No, it's a bird.' 'No.' They all groaned. 'It's Burper.'

Miss wasn't standing any nonsense. She marched to the window. She threw it open.

'Come inside and sit down. Roderick. Immediately.'

The breeze wafted Burper in across the classroom. His head went clonk on the opposite wall. Two of the lads helpfully reached up with their rulers and pushed him off. Away he went across the space between floor and ceiling.

'Shut the window,' ordered Miss quickly. The window was shut just as Burper tapped against it. Miss marched out from her desk again and got hold of Burper's wind-cheater and dragged him back down to his place. She got him sat down – which took some pushing and pulling, but no sooner had she stepped back and said, 'Now Roderick, just what do you think you are playing at?' when up he popped again and started spinning slowly round. Every time Miss tried to grasp him, he spun away again. He was getting so dizzy he couldn't see straight. Now several lads and girls joined in, trying to help. At least that's what they reckoned they were doing. But in fact it only made matters worse. It was like a gigantic balloon game. Before long the classroom was in chaos with everyone joining in. It was more fun than sports day, more fun than the Christmas Party, more fun than the time the tents came down at the school camp. It was hilarious. It was a riot.

It might have gone on for ever, well, till lunch time at least, but then something quite unexpected happened.

Djamila stood up and called, 'Burper.'

Burper stopped whirling round in the air and looked down.

'Drop the lamp!'

He dropped the lamp and Djamila caught it neatly.

While everyone watched open-mouthed, she raised the lamp in the air and spoke very clearly and slowly in another language.

There was a whistling sound and a terrific crash as Burper dropped like a stone on top of a desk. It bent, but it didn't break, fortunately. Miss helped Burper up on to his feet and took him out to Nurse to get his bumps seen to. In all the noise and confusion no one noticed, until Miss came back, that Djamila had gone.

Next day, the class heard that her family had

moved away. Everyone was sorry, because life was just that little bit slower and duller now Djamila wasn't there.

No one was more sorry than Burper. For weeks he didn't talk to anyone. Not even 'Gimme that,' or 'I'll thump you.' He never explained how he'd come to be floating like a balloon across the classroom that day. And Miss decided there was no point in trying to find out.

The old lamp had gone too, so that rather scrubbed round Aladdin for the Christmas Play. Miss had to think of something fairly quickly, so people could choose the parts and start rehearsing.

Burper wasn't seen in the dining hall for weeks. He was spotted lurking round the school yard with a packet of crispbread and a tomato. And once or twice, lads and girls who had newspaper rounds spotted him jogging round the park, puffing away to himself.

Miss chose *Cinderella*. Burper, who had lost two stone, got the part of Buttons. You wouldn't chuckle! But he didn't seem to mind. He did it rather well.

He's stopped thumping people – well no more than average, anyway. He's stopped burping in class. But that's the trouble with nicknames. This one's stuck to him.

But he's in better condition now. And anyone who calls him Burper to his face had better have twenty yards start.

Time Trouble

by Penelope Lively
Chosen by Lindsey Fraser
Executive Director, Book Trust Scotland

When I was nine I came to an arrangement with a grandfather clock; it was disastrous. Never trust a clock. Believe me – I know. I'll tell you about it.

I was in the hall of our house, all by myself. Except for the clock. I'd just come in from school. The clock said ten past four. And I said, out loud, because I was fed up and cross as two sticks, 'I'd give anything to have this afternoon all over again.'

'Would you now,' said a voice. 'That's interesting.' There was no one there. I swear. Mum was out shopping and my brother Brian was off playing with his mate down the road. The voice came from the clock. I looked it in the eye and it looked back, the way they do. Well, they've got faces, haven't they? Faces look.

'I deal in time, as it happens,' the clock went on. 'Had some bad time, have you?'

Funny stuff, time. I mean, it can be good or bad, and you're always being told not to lose it and we all spend it and some of us kill it. You can have overtime and half-time and summer time and the time of your life. And there's always next time. And my time's my own, so's yours.

I nodded.

'Sometimes,' said the clock, 'I can lend a hand.' It twitched one, from eleven minutes past four to twelve minutes past. 'Tell me all, then.'

So I told. About how at dinner I was in a bad mood because of having a fight with Brian and when Mum kept going on at me about something I kept thinking 'Oh, shut up!' only unfortunately what was meant to be a think got said out loud accidentally so then Mum was in a very bad mood indeed with me and I

110

got no pudding. And then on the way back to school Brian and I had another fight and my new pencil case got kicked into a puddle and all dirtied over. And we were late and Mrs Harris told us off. And I answered back accidentally and so she sent me to the headmaster and he told me off even more. And I had to stay in at break. And Martin Chalmers nicked my rubber so I had to keep asking for it back so Mrs Harris told me off again. And I had to go to the end of the classroom and sit by myself. And on the way home I got hold of Martin Chalmers and we had an argument resulting in my falling over and my pocket money dropping out of my pocket and ten pence getting lost.

'Tough,' said the clock. 'I see what you mean. Well – here's a deal. You have this afternoon back and I'll have next Wednesday.'

'Next Wednesday?'

'Next Wednesday. Your next Wednesday afternoon.'

'But I don't know yet what's going to happen next Wednesday,' I objected.

'Quite,' said the clock. 'It's a risk. Well – take it or leave it.'

I thought. What's one Wednesday afternoon, out of all the Wednesday afternoons you've got? I mean, on the whole one Wednesday afternoon's much like another.

'O.K,' I said. 'And I have this one again?'

The clock made its whirring noise for quarter past four. 'That's right, my lad. See if you can make a better job of it.'

You're not going to believe this. There I was at dinner all over again, in a bad mood just like before,

only this time when Mum started going on at me I
didn't say anything. I just sat. And then somehow
accidentally my leg shot out and it kicked Brian and
Brian yelled and his milk got spilled and Mum got in
a proper temper and not only did I get no pudding
but I got no seconds either. On the way back to
school I thought. Right . . . And when Brian started
trying to trip me up I didn't trip back but I started

running on ahead. And a paving stone got in my way and I fell over and my new pencil case went into the road and a car went over it and all the pencils were broken and the biro with six colours was bent so it wouldn't work any more. And we were late and I didn't answer Mrs Harris back but I kept trying to explain only she called it interrupting and the headmaster came in and heard and I had to stay in at break and help tidy up the infant class as a punishment and Brian and Martin Chalmers kept looking in at the window and making faces and I made faces back. And I got on one of the desks to see out better. And put dirty footmarks on it. And Mrs Harris came in. So I had to spend all afternoon at the end of the classroom by myself. And when the bell went I rushed off before Martin Chalmers came out and I was so fed up I went into the corner shop for a Twix. And you're not going to believe this. My money had all gone out of my pocket. Twenty-eight pence from last Sunday. It must have dropped out when I fell over before.

There I was in the hall again. With the clock. Furious. I said, 'It was *worse*. I want the first one back again. That way, at least I'd have my money and the pencils and the biro with six colours.'

'No way,' said the clock. 'A deal's a deal.' And it just stood there, ticking. That was all it did for the next five days.

I wondered what would happen, when it came to Wednesday. What happened was this. Brian and I came home from school for dinner, just as usual. We ate it, just as usual. Mum said, 'Off you go, boys,' just as usual. We started getting on our anoraks. The phone rang. The clock struck one. Mum said, 'Wonder who that is . . .' She went to answer the phone.

. . . And the next thing I knew the clock was striking seven and I was in the kitchen again looking at a plate of supper that I didn't want. I felt a bit sick.

I said, 'I feel a bit sick.'

'I'm not surprised,' said Mum.

'You shouldn't have had the peach melba bombs as well as the vanilla with chocolate sauce,' said Brian.

I looked at him.

'Cor . . .' he went on, in a sort of contented reflective voice. 'Weren't the Jumbo Beefburgers *smashing* . . .'

I didn't say a word. An awful, suspicious feeling began to creep over me.

Brian was talking about something else now. 'Remember the bit when the spaceships all started crashing into each other? That was *fantastic*. And when the robots all came out of the volcano?'

Mum had gone out of the back door for something. I thought hard. I said, cautiously, 'What sort of an afternoon was it, would you say?'

'What sort of an afternoon!' cried Brian. 'It was just amazing! Well, you were *there*, you dope! I mean, it's not just any old afternoon that Uncle Jim suddenly rings up and says he's over this way and he'd like to take us out and he talks Mum into letting us miss school and he comes in his new *sports* car with the *roof* down all the way and . . . Well, you were *there*. Hey – remember the bit in the cartoon when they all fell over the cliff!'

I swallowed. 'Yeah . . . Sure.' After a moment I

said, 'It was *Space Victory*, was it, the film?'

He stared at me. "Course it was *Space Victory*, idiot. *Space Victory*, what we've been wanting to see for *years*. Remember the bit when . . .'

"Course,' I snarled through clenched teeth. I went on, wishing I wasn't, 'What's that place called – the Wimpy Bar, is it?'

'Wimpy Bar!' cried Brian. 'Some Wimpy Bar! That was the Plaza Steak House, you nut! Hey – bet you haven't ever had three helpings of chips before!'

I groaned. I wished he'd shut up, but I went on listening.

'*And* beefburgers *and* bacon rolls *and* Coca Cola *and* three different kinds of ice cream *and* crisps *and* milk shakes. Actually,' he said, pushing his plate to one side, 'I feel a tiny bit sick too. I'll just *think* about it all. Remember the bit when . . .'

I went out into the hall, banging the door. I stood in front of the clock. 'Did you *know*?' I demanded.

'What's that?' said the clock, bland as you like.

'Did you *know* that it wouldn't just be an ordinary school afternoon? Did you *know* Uncle Jim would come . . . and . . . *Space Victory* . . . *three* helpings of chips . . .' I spluttered. I couldn't go on.

The clock ticked away, evasive. 'I said it would be a risk, didn't I! Funny stuff, time. Doesn't always do to mess about with it.'

'It was your idea,' I said sulkily.

'Look,' said the clock. 'I was just going about my normal business, dealing in time. If you don't like what's in the paper you don't complain to the newsagent, do you?'

I glared at it.

'I just keep track of it, right? See it's moving along at the proper rate, all that kind of thing. One bit's the same as another, far as I'm concerned. The quality's your problem – doesn't interest me.'

I said, 'I want my Wednesday afternoon back.'

The clock considered. 'Mmm. That would be a new arrangement. Different deal altogether. Let's see now. How about next, um, next December the twenty-fifth?'

'*Christmas Day?*' I yelled.

'Suit yourself.' If a clock can be said to shrug, it did so. I thought about *Space Victory* and Uncle Jim's sports car with the roof down and three different kinds of ice cream. I mean, the whole point about having a good time is that it's good when you have it and it's still good when you remember it. And I couldn't remember any of this; I'd had it and not known about it then and I still don't know about it. I thought about next Christmas. Half the point of good things that are going to come is that you know you've still got them coming. No, the clock wasn't going to get Christmas.

'Tomorrow morning?' I offered. After all, an ordinary old Thursday morning . . .

'I've got lots of those,' said the clock.

'I thought you said it was all the same to you?' I said craftily.

'Cheeky!' snapped the clock. 'You watch out or I'll stop. And then where will you be?'

I didn't know the answer to that, so I said nothing. 'Tell you what. I'll be generous. I'll just have the time you waste. Now that you'll never miss.'

I thought. I thought, I bet there's a snag somewhere.

116

I didn't trust that clock an inch now. After a moment I said, 'O.K. But just for next week.'

'You're so sharp you'll cut yourself. A month.'

'Two weeks.'

The clock whirred. 'All right, then. Done. Off you go. Have fun.'

And it struck one and there I was in the kitchen and the phone was ringing and Mum saying, 'Wonder who that is . . .'

And Uncle Jim came and he took us off in the sports car with the roof down and we went to *Space Victory* and then to Plaza Steak House and I had two Jumbo Beefburgers and three helpings of chips and three different kinds of ice cream and Coca Cola and . . . It was all exactly like I knew it was going to be. Oh, yes, it was pretty good, I mean it was fantastic in a way but the edge had kind of gone off it. It wasn't nearly as fantastic as it ought to have been. Half the point of a good time is not knowing what's coming next. So *Space Victory* wasn't as amazing as I though it was going to be and the beefburgers were all right but not much more and I kept thinking it wasn't as good as it was supposed to be which made it worse.

And I was stuck with the deal. I bet you're wondering about that. So was I. I mean, who's to say whether you're wasting time or not? Mothers and teachers have one idea about wasting time; people like me have another. Fact is, if you're anything like me you probably do quite a lot of smooching around doing nothing in particular, sort of waiting for something to happen. I s'pose you *could* call that wasting time, if you insisted.

The clock, evidently, did. It was the worst two

weeks I've ever had. I'm telling you. Every time I stopped doing something, such as eating a meal or having a bath or doing maths or walking to school or getting dressed, everything just went blank. And there I'd be again in the middle of the next thing. It was like being in a speeded-up film. It was all go; there was never a moment's peace. I was exhausted. There I'd be cleaning my teeth and I'd dawdle a bit and try out a few faces in the bathroom mirror and then wham! I'd find myself downstairs and out of the front door on the way to school. Or I'd stop in the middle of a sum to have a bit of a think and the think would begin to get sort of vague and wandery – you know the way they do – and whoosh! there I'd be sweating away again at the sum and the bell would be going for break. I didn't know if I was coming or going. The only thing to be said for it was that the days went by double-quick. Suddenly the two weeks were over and everything slowed up and went back to normal. Goodness – what a relief! The first thing I did was go into the hall and stand in front of the clock and do absolutely nothing, for five whole minutes, on purpose. I'd have gone on longer, just to annoy it, except that I was getting bored. I started to go upstairs.

'All right,' said the clock. 'You've made your point.'

I glared at the clock and the clock looked back, blank. No, not blank: smug.

'Look,' it said. 'Maybe I could interest you in a personal arrangement. Just you and me. Might be fun. How about you . . .'

'NO!' I shouted.

William's Version
by Jan Mark
Chosen by Elizabeth Hammill
Children's Books Manager, Waterstone's, Newcastle

William and Granny were left to entertain each other for an hour while William's mother went to the clinic.

'Sing to me,' said William.

'Granny's too old to sing,' said Granny.

'I'll sing to you then,' said William. William only knew one song. He had forgotten the words and the tune, but he sang it several times, anyway.

'Shall we do something else now?' said Granny.

'Tell me a story,' said William. 'Tell me about the wolf.'

'Red Riding Hood?'

'No, not *that* wolf, the other wolf.'

'Peter and the wolf?' said Granny.

'Mummy's going to have a baby,' said William.

'I know,' said Granny.

William looked suspicious.

'How do you know?'

'Well . . . she told me. And it shows, doesn't it?'

'The lady down the road had a baby. It looks like a pig,' said William. He counted on his fingers. 'Three babies looks like three pigs.'

'Ah,' said Granny. 'Once upon a time there were three little pigs. Their names were –'

'They didn't have names,' said William.

'Yes they did. The first pig was called –'

'Pigs don't have names.'

'Some do. These pigs had names.'

'No they didn't.' William slid off Granny's lap and went to open the corner cupboard by the fireplace. Old magazines cascaded out as old magazines do when they have been flung into a cupboard and the door slammed shut. He rooted among them until he found a little book covered with brown paper, climbed into the cupboard, opened the book, closed it and climbed out again. 'They didn't have names,' he said.

'I didn't know you could read,' said Granny, properly impressed.

'C – A – T, wheelbarrow,' said William.

'Is that the book Mummy reads to you out of?'

'It's my book,' said William.

'But it's the one Mummy reads?'

'If she says please,' said William.

'Well, that's Mummy's story, then. My pigs have names.'

'They're the wrong pigs.' William was not open to negotiation. 'I don't want them in this story.'

'Can't we have different pigs this time?'

'No. They won't know what to do.'

'Once upon a time,' said Granny, 'there were three little pigs who lived with their mother.'

'Their mother was dead,' said William.

'Oh, I'm sure she wasn't,' said Granny.

'She was dead. You make bacon out of dead pigs. She got eaten for breakfast and they threw the rind out for the birds.'

'So the three little pigs had to find homes for themselves.'

'No.' William consulted his book. 'They had to build little houses.'

'I'm just coming to that.'

'You said they had to *find* homes. They didn't *find* them.'

'The first little pig walked along for a bit until he met a man with a load of hay.'

'It was a lady.'

'A lady with a load of hay?'

'NO! It was a lady-pig. You said *he.*'

'I thought all the pigs were little boy-pigs,' said Granny.

'It says lady-pig here,' said William. 'It says the lady-pig went for a walk and met a man with a load of hay.'

'So the lady-pig,' said Granny, 'said to the man, "May I have some of that hay to build a house?" and the man said, "Yes." Is that right?'

'Yes,' said William. 'You know that baby?'

'What baby?'

'The one Mummy's going to have. Will that baby have shoes on when it comes out?'

'I don't think so,' said Granny.

'It will have cold feet,' said William.

'Oh no,' said Granny. 'Mummy will wrap it up in a soft shawl, all snug.'

'I don't *mind* if it has cold feet,' William explained. 'Go on about the lady-pig.'

'So the little lady-pig took the hay and built a little house. Soon the wolf came along and the wolf said –'

'You didn't tell where the wolf lived.'

'I don't know where the wolf lived.'

'15 Tennyson Avenue, next to the bomb-site,' said William.

'I bet it doesn't say that in the book,' said Granny, with spirit.

'Yes it does.'

'Let me see, then.'

William folded himself up with his back to Granny, and pushed the book up under his pullover.

'*I* don't think it says that in the book,' said Granny.

'It's in ever so small words,' said William.

'So the wolf said, "Little pig, little pig, let me come in," and the little pig answered, "No." So the wolf said, "Then I'll huff and I'll puff and I'll blow your house down," and he huffed and he puffed and he blew the house down, and the little pig ran away.'

'He ate the little pig,' said William.

'No, no,' said Granny. 'The little pig ran away.'

'He ate the little pig. He ate her in a sandwich.'

'All right, he ate the little pig in a sandwich. So the second little pig –'

'You didn't tell about the tricycle.'

'What about the tricycle?'

'The wolf got on his tricycle and went to the bread shop to buy some bread. To make the sandwich,' William explained, patiently.

'Oh well, the wolf got on his tricycle and went to the bread shop to buy some bread. And he went to the grocer's to buy some butter.' This innovation did not go down well.

'He already had some butter in the cupboard,' said William.

'So then the second little pig went for a walk and met a man with a load of wood, and the little pig said to the man, "May I have some of that wood to build a house?" and the man said, "Yes".'

'He didn't say please.'

' "Please may I have some of that wood to build a house?" '

'It was sticks.'

'Sticks *are* wood.'

William took out his book and turned the pages. 'That's right,' he said.

'Why don't you tell the story?' said Granny.

'I can't remember it,' said William.

'You could read it out of your book.'

'I've lost it,' said William, clutching his pullover. 'Look, do you know who this is?' He pulled a green angora scarf from under the sofa.

'No, who is it?' said Granny, glad of the diversion.

'This is Doctor Snake.' He made the scarf wriggle across the carpet.

'Why is he a doctor?'

'Because he is all furry,' said William. He wrapped the doctor round his neck and sat sucking the loose end. 'Go on about the wolf.'

'So the little pig built a house of sticks and along came the wolf – on his tricycle?'

'He came by bus. He didn't have any money for a ticket so he ate up the conductor.'

'That wasn't very nice of him,' said Granny.

'No,' said William. 'It wasn't *very* nice.'

'And the wolf said, "Little pig, little pig, let me come in," and the little pig said, "No," and the wolf said, "Then I'll huff and I'll puff and I'll blow your house down." And then what did he do?' Granny asked, cautiously.

William was silent.

'Did he eat the second little pig?'

'Yes.'

'How did he eat this little pig?' said Granny, prepared for more pig sandwiches or possibly pig on toast.

'With his mouth,' said William.

'Now the third little pig went for a walk and met a man with a load of bricks. And the little pig said, "*Please* may I have some of those bricks to build a house?" and the man said, "Yes." So the little pig took the bricks and built a house.'

'He built it on the bomb-site.'

'Next door to the wolf?' said Granny. 'That was very silly of him.'

'There wasn't anywhere else,' said William. 'All the roads were full up.'

'The wolf didn't have to come by bus or tricycle this time, then, did he?' said Granny, grown cunning.

'Yes.' William took out the book and peered in, secretively. 'He was playing in the cemetery. He had to get another bus.

'And did he eat the conductor this time?'

'No. A nice man gave him some money, so he bought a ticket.'

'I'm glad to hear it,' said Granny.

'He ate the nice man,' said William.

'So the wolf got off the bus and went up to the little pig's house, and he said, "Little pig, little pig, let me come in," and the little pig said, "No," and then the wolf said, "I'll huff and I'll puff and I'll blow your house down," and he huffed and he puffed and he huffed and he puffed but he couldn't blow the house down because it was made of bricks.'

'He couldn't blow it down,' said William, 'because it was stuck to the ground.'

'Well, anyway, the wolf got very cross then, and he climbed on the roof and shouted down the chimney, "I'm coming to get you!" but the little pig just laughed and put a big saucepan of water on the fire.'

'He put it on the gas stove.'

'He put it on the *fire*,' said Granny, speaking very rapidly, 'and the wolf fell down the chimney and into

126

the pan of water and was boiled and the little pig ate him for supper.'

William threw himself full length on the carpet and screamed.

'He didn't! He didn't! He *didn't!* He didn't eat the wolf.'

Granny picked him up, all stiff and kicking, and sat him on her lap.

'Did I get it wrong again, love? Don't cry. Tell me what really happened.'

William wept, and wiped his nose on Doctor Snake.

'The little pig put the saucepan on the gas stove and the wolf got down the chimney and put the little pig in the saucepan and boiled him. He had him for tea, with chips,' said William.

'Oh,' said Granny. 'I've got it all wrong, haven't I? Can I see the book, then I shall know, next time.'

William took the book from under his pullover. Granny opened it and read, *First Aid for Beginners: a Practical Handbook.*

'I see,' said Granny. 'I don't think I can read this. I left my glasses at home. You tell Gran how it ends.'

William turned to the last page which showed a prostrate man with his leg in a splint; *compound fracture of the femur.*

'Then the wolf washed up and got on his tricycle and went to see his Granny, and his Granny opened the door and said, "Hello, William."'

'I thought it was the wolf.'

'It was. It was the wolf. His name was William Wolf,' said William.

'What a nice story,' said Granny. 'You tell it much

better than I do.'

'I can see up your nose,' said William. 'It's all whiskery.'

What's for Dinner?

by Robert Swindells
Chosen by Valerie Bierman
Children's Fair Organiser, Edinburgh Book Festival

'It's Friday,' Sammy Troy complained. 'Fish and chip day. Why are we having shepherd's pie?'

'I don't know, do I?' said Jane. They were twins but Sammy was ten minutes younger and ten years dafter. Jane spent half her time at school keeping him out of trouble. She swallowed a forkful of the pie. 'It's very tasty anyway. Try it.'

Sammy tried it. It was good, but he wasn't going to admit it. He'd been looking forward to fish and chips and shepherd's pie just wasn't the same. He pulled a face.

'Pigfood.'

'Don't be silly,' said Jane, but she knew he would be. He usually was.

Sammy left most of his dinner, and in the playground afterwards he made up a rap. It was about the school cook, and it went like this:

'Elsie Brook is a useless cook
If you eat school dinners it's your hard luck
They either kill or make you ill
If the meat don't do it then the custard will.'

It wasn't true. Mrs Brook did good dinners, but the rap caught on and a long snake of chanting children wound its way about the playground with Sammy at its head. Jane didn't join in. She thought it was stupid and hoped Mrs Brook wouldn't hear it.

On Saturday, Sammy practised the rap with some of his friends. They meant to get it going again at break on Monday, but at the end of morning assembly the head said, 'I'm sorry to have to tell you all that our Mrs Brook was taken ill over the

130

weekend and will not be here to cook for us this week.'

Some of the boys grinned and nudged one another. Sammy whispered in Jane's ear, 'She must've eaten some of that shepherd's pie.' Jane jabbed him with her elbow.

'However,' continued the head, 'we are very lucky to have with us Mr Hannay, who will see to our meals till Mrs Brook returns. Mr Hannay is not only a first-class chef but an explorer as well. He has travelled as cook on a number of expeditions to remote regions, and is famous for his ability to produce appetising meals from the most unpromising ingredients.'

'He'll feel at home here, then,' muttered Sammy. 'We have the most unpromising ingredients in Europe.'

A chef, though! A first-class chef. Morning lessons seemed to drag on forever. It felt like three o'clock when the buzzer went, though it was five to twelve as always. Hands were washed in two seconds flat, and everybody hurried along to the dining area which was filled with a delicious mouth-watering aroma. Snowy cloths covered all the tables, and on each table stood a little pot of flowers. 'Wow!' breathed Jeanette Frazer. 'It's like a posh restaurant.'

And the food. Oh, the food. First came a thick, fragrant soup which was green but tasted absolutely fantastic. To follow the soup there was a beautiful main course – succulent nuggets of tender white meat in a golden, spicy sauce with baby peas and crispy roast potatoes. And for pudding there were giant helpings of chocolate ice cream with crunchy bits in it.

Sammy licked the last smear of ice cream from his spoon, dropped the spoon in his dish, pushed the dish away and belched. Some of the boys giggled, but his sister glared at him across the table. Sammy smiled. 'Sorry, but what a meal, eh? What a stupendous pig-out. I'll probably nod off in biology this aft.'

He didn't though. Miss Corbishley didn't give him the chance. The class was doing pond life, and when they walked in the room the teacher said, 'Jane and Sammy Troy, take the net and specimen jar, go down to the pond and bring back some pond beetles and a water boatman or two. Quickly now.'

The school pond lay in a hollow beyond the playing field. Rushes grew thickly round its marshy rim and there were tadpoles, newts and dragonflies as well as sticklebacks and the beetles they'd study today. It was Sammy's favourite spot, but today all the creatures seemed to be hiding. No dragonflies darted away as the twins waded through the reeds. No sticklebacks scattered like silver pins when Jane trawled the net through the pondweed, and when she lifted it out it was empty.

'Try again,' said Sammy. 'Faster.'

Jane sent the net swooping through the under-water forest, but all she got was a plume of weed.

'Everything seems to have done,' she said. 'And Miss is waiting.'

'I know,' said Sammy. 'She'll think we've wagged off school.

'Don't be ridiculous!' cried Miss Corbishley, when Jane told her there was nothing in the pond. 'Only this morning Mr Hannay was saying what a well-stocked pond we have at Milton Middle.' The twins were sent to their seats in disgrace, while Jeannette Frazer and Mary Bain went to try their luck. Miss Corbishley made a giant drawing of a water boatman on the board and the children began copying it into their books.

'Hey, Jane!' hissed Sammy. His sister looked at him. He had a funny look on his face. 'I've just had a thought.

'Congratulations,' she whispered. 'I knew you would some day.'

'No, listen. You know what Miss said, about Mr Hannay?'

'What about it?'

'He said the pond was well stocked, right? And now it isn't. And we had that fantastic dinner, only we didn't really know what it was?'

'What's dinner got to do with – ?' Jane broke off and gazed at her brother. She shook her head. 'No, Sammy. No. That's sick. It's impossible.'

'Is it?' Sammy jabbed a finger at her. 'What was that soup, then? Green soup. And the meat. And those crunchy bits in the ice cream – what were they?'

Before Jane could reply, Jeanette and Mary came back with long faces and an empty jar.

Walking home that afternoon Jane said, 'It's a coincidence, that's all. It can't be true what you're thinking, Sammy.' She wasn't sure though, and Sammy certainly wasn't convinced. 'I wonder what we'll get tomorrow?' he said.

Tuesday's dinner turned out to be every bit as delicious as Monday's. The twins had kept their suspicions to themselves, so there were no spoilt appetites as the children settled down to eat. Even Jane and Sammy felt better. After all, even Mr Hannay couldn't conjure food from an empty pond.

The soup was orange and there were no lumps in it. It had plenty of flavour though, and everybody enjoyed it. The main course was Italian – mounds of steaming pasta and a rich, meaty tomato sauce. 'If this is how they eat in Italy,' said Sammy, 'I'm off to live there.' He seemed to have forgotten about yesterday. Jane hadn't, but she knew macaroni when she saw it, and this was definitely macaroni.

Tuesday afternoon was C.D.T. with Mr Parker. When the kids arrived he was kneeling in front of his big cupboard, surrounded by a mountain of dusty old drawings, and broken models made from balsa wood and cardboard boxes. 'Lost something, sir?' asked Sammy.

Mr Parker nodded. 'I'm afraid I have, lad. I couldn't sworn they were in here.'

'What, sir?'

'Some pictures I did with a first-year class three, maybe four years ago. Collage pictures.'

'What are they, sir?'

'Oh, you know – you stick things on a sheet of paper to make a picture. Seashells, lentils, bits of macaroni. Any old rubbish you can find, really.'

Sammy gulped. 'Bits of macaroni, sir?'

'That's right.'

'Four years ago, sir?'

'Yes. I'm sure I saw them at the back of the

cupboard quite recently and made a mental note to clear them out before the mice got to them.'

'Are there mice in your cupboard, sir?' There was a greenish tint to Sammy's face.

'Oh yes, lad. Mice, moths, woodlice, cockroaches. The odd rat, probably. It's a miniature zoo, this cupboard.'

Sammy didn't enjoy C.D.T. that afternoon. He couldn't concentrate. He kept picturing old Hannay in his blue and white striped apron, rooting through Parker's cupboard. When he glanced across at Jane he thought she looked unwell. He wondered how Mrs Brook was getting along, and when the boys did the rap at break he didn't join in.

On Wednesday, Jane and Sammy decided they wouldn't eat school lunch unless they knew what it was. Sammy said, 'How do we find out what it is?'

'We ask,' Jane told him. At eleven o'clock she stuck her hand up and asked to go to the toilet but went to the kitchen instead. Mr Hannay wasn't there, but Mrs Trafford was. 'Where's Mr Hannay?' asked Jane. She hoped he'd left, but Mrs Trafford said, 'He's just slipped along to the gym, dear. Why – who wants him?'

'Oh, nobody,' said Jane. 'I was wondering what's for dinner, that's all.'

'Opek,' said Mrs Trafford.

'Pardon?' said Jane.

'Opek. It's a very old oriental dish, Mr Hannay says. Very nice.'

Opek turned out to be a grey, porridge mush. It

didn't look all that promising, but it was probably what ancient oriental grub was supposed to look like and it tasted fine. Everybody was enjoying it till Gaz Walker fished a small flat rectangular object from his plate and held it up.

'Here,' he complained. 'Why is there a Size 4 tag in my dinner?'

'Let's have a look.' Jane took the tag and examined it. It looked like the sort of tag you'd find inside a shoe. 'Opek,' she murmured, wondering why Mr Hannay had been in the gym when he was supposed to be cooking. 'Opek.' An idea formed in her head and sank slowly into her stomach where it lay like a lead weight. She put the tag on the rim of her plate and sat back with her hands across her stomach. All round the table, kids stopped eating and watched her.

'What's up, Jane?' Sammy's voice was husky.

'Opek,' whispered Jane. 'I think I know what it means.'

'What does it mean?' asked Jeanette, who had almost cleared her plate.

'I think it's initials,' said Jane. 'Standing for Old P.E. Kit.'

The peace of the dining area was shattered by cries of revulsion and the scrape and clatter of chairs as everybody on Jane's table stampeded for the door. The kids at the other tables watched till they'd gone, then lowered their heads and went on eating opek.

Sometimes two people can keep a secret, but never ten. There were ten kids at Jane and Sammy's table, and so the secret came out. Nobody went in to dinner on Thursday. Nobody. At twelve o'clock Mr Hannay raised the hatch and found himself gazing at twelve empty tables. He frowned at his watch. Shook it. Raised it to his ear. At five-past twelve he took off his apron and went to see the head. They stood at the head's window, looking toward the playing field. All the children were there, and some seemed to be eating the grass. 'Good lord,' sighed the head. 'What did you cook, Hannay?'

'Epsatsc,' said the chef.

'Never heard of it,' said the head. 'What is it?'

'Traditional Greek dish,' said Hannay smoothly, easily fooling the head. Jane, who'd got the word from Mrs Trafford, wasn't fooled. 'Epsatsc' she said, grimly, leaning on a goalpost. 'Erasers, pencil shavings and the school cat.'

On Friday everybody brought sandwiches but they needn't have, because Hannay had gone and Mrs Brook was back. When they spotted her crossing the playground at five to nine the kids cheered. Mrs Brook, who was the sentimental type, had to wipe her eyes before she could see to hang up her coat. The kids chucked their butties in the bin and Sammy's rap was dead.

Dinner wasn't fish and chips, but there were no complaints. Everybody tucked in with gusto – even Sammy. The snowy cloths had gone and there were no flowers, but there was something else instead. Contentment. You could feel it all around.

And so the school week drew to a close. Everybody relaxed. The work was done. The weekend, bright with promise, lay ahead. At half-past three the kids spilled whooping into the yard and away down the drive. Jane and Sammy, in no rush, strolled behind.

138

At the top of the drive stood the gardener, looking lost. Sammy grinned. 'What's up, Mr Tench?' The gardener lifted his cap and scratched his head. 'Nay,' he growled. 'There were a pile of nice, fresh horse manure here this morning and it's gone.'

The twins exchanged glances. Mrs Brook was coming down the drive. They ran to her. 'Mrs Brook!' cried Sammy. 'That Mr Hannay – he has left, hasn't he?'

The cook nodded. 'Yes, dear, I'm afraid he has but don't worry – he left me his recipe book, and you know it's just amazing the meals you can get out of stuff you find lying around.'